# WHEN LIFE CHANGES DIRECTION

By

## CHRISTINE FRIEND

To Jacqui,

Best Wishes

Christine x

*Cover graphics by*

*Louis Hood*

*Also by, Christine Friend*

*Living With The Consequences*

Copyright © Christine Friend 2021

# Part One

## *Chapter One*

19th January 1934

The Doctor was tired; exasperated and irritated by his patient's husband.
"Mr Bailey, your wife has had a difficult labour. She hasn't given birth to one baby but two. She needs help and looking after. The babies are only twenty four hours old."
"Look, Doctor, I have paid you your money. My Mum lives here with us she'll help. It's woman's work and I am due back on ship the day after tomorrow. I'll get them registered and wet their heads, then I'm off. Two more mouths to feed and not one of them a son!"
Doctor White bent down to pick up his bag. He turned to pick his hat up off the dressing table and bid good day to Agnes Bailey, the exhausted woman lying in the bed. Tommy, her husband, followed the Doctor downstairs and saw him off the premises.
The house was a rented mid terrace, two up and two down in Stepney, East London. It had no bathroom inside, but they were lucky they had their own privy outside the back door. The house wasn't old, it was early Edwardian, but had always been a rented property so no repairs had been done since the day the house had been built.
Tommy called to his Mother that he was off to get the babies registered, and would be back for his tea at 5

o'clock. His Mother, Sarah, was a small, fragile looking woman in her early sixties, she rose from the hard chair she was sitting on.

She looked much older than her years. Life had been hard for her. She had married Harry Bailey at 21, and after many years of trying and hoping for a baby, she had given birth to Tommy when she was nearly 40. She had doted on her son, but he had grown up to be a callous and hard man. She had always said he turned that way when his Father died and had to start taking responsibility, but anyone who knew Tommy knew that responsibly wasn't his strong point. At 21 he had joined the navy - 6 months after his Father had died. Then, on his first leave, he married Agnes; a kind young lady of 23, who was a neighbour of the Bailey's. She was a dressmaker, hard-working and reliable, and she worked hard to supplement the money that Tommy sent home for them.

Tommy eventually arrived home much later than he had told his Mother, and a little bit the worse for drink. He threw his coat on the back of the worn arm chair, and called to his Mother for his tea.

Mrs Bailey was upstairs with Agnes and her Granddaughters. She heard Tommy call out as he slammed the front door and woke both babies who had only just been put down to sleep. She handed them both to Agnes, and then made her way downstairs. Mrs Bailey had suffered with arthritis for a number of years and although she was trying to hurry, negotiating the stairs was a slow process for her. By the time she reached the front room, Tommy was sound asleep in the armchair. She walked slowly to the scullery, where she had been keeping his tea warm on a plate over a saucepan of steaming water. She turned the gas off. It was nearly 9.30pm - she didn't expect Tommy to wake up until morning. She used the privy, and then heated some milk for Agnes and herself. With this, she made her way very slowly upstairs.

When Mrs Bailey awoke the next morning, her bedroom was bitterly cold. There was no form of heating in the little bedroom. She eased herself off the thin mattress, and reached for her shawl, which she put around her shoulders. Quietly, she opened the door on to the little landing and made her way to see her daughter in law, and the babies.
All was quiet. Agnes lay fast asleep. Mrs. Bailey crept over to the cot, where both babies were also sleeping. Looking back at Agnes, she felt sad. The day her son had brought his new wife to the house, their wedding day, she was blooming with happiness. No one would be in any doubt that Agnes had married Tommy for love, but most would say Tommy had been lucky with his choice of bride. Agnes was tall, slim and would have looked sensational in the clothes that she made for the high end market. But it was her face that drew people to her. It was oval, with big grey eyes, a full mouth, beautiful smile, and masses of brown, shiny, curly hair. Looking at Agnes now, it was hard for Mrs Bailey to recognise her as the same person. The shiny hair was dull, she had black bags around her eyes. Her face was sunken, and at 24, already had lines.

Christine Friend

Agnes opened her eyes to see Mrs Bailey looking at her. She was startled, and spoke,
"The babies, they are alright?"
Mrs Bailey whispered back,
"They are both fine. Why don't you pop down and have a wash in the scullery and I'll stay up here and keep an eye on them?"
"That would be lovely", she replied.
Agnes grabbed a clean nightie that she had recently made, and took herself downstairs.
As she passed the front room, she could hear Tommy gently snoring. She went into the scullery, filled the kettle and lit the gas ring with a match and placed the kettle over it. Then, she went out into the bitter cold morning to use the privy. Fifteen minutes later she had had a wash. She left the nightie she had taken off in soak in a bowl. This meant more washing for her Mother-in-law, who was already struggling with the extra work. She then refilled the kettle to make a pot of tea for everyone.
While waiting for the kettle to boil she went to see if Tommy was awake. She was hoping he had managed to register the babies births.
Tommy was still asleep, but in his coat she could see some paper work hanging out of the pocket. She took it out, and read the birth details of her daughters. To her shock, Tommy had registered them as Margaret and Margery.
She started to feel faint, and managed to sit herself down on the hard chair. She didn't pass out, but, began to cry. The noise woke Tommy.

## When Life Changes Direction

"What's the matter Aggie? you've woken me up! Ooh my head."

"Tommy, what have you done? We decided that the girls would be called Isobel, and Daisy. Instead, you registered them as Margaret and Margery?!"

"Well, when I was in the pub, we all thought Isabel and Daisy sounded too posh, and anyway, what's wrong with Margaret? It's good enough for the King and Queen. Look Aggie, some of your ideas, well, they're above us. Oh stop crying, you know I can't stand it!" He stood up.

"Look, I am going back to me ship today. It's probably for the best, and then you and me Mum can get on with things."

## *Chapter Two*

31$^{st}$ August 1939

"Mummy, I don't want to go!"
Margery was crying, and her Mother could barely understand what she was saying. Agnes picked her up and sat down in the armchair with her.
 Margery's twin sister was standing in the door way, not really understanding why her sister was making so much fuss. Tomorrow, they were being taken by their Mother to their school. From there, they were getting on a bus to the railway station and then on a train. Their Mother said they were being evacuated, and that it was just like a holiday, but they had never had one of those - although it did sound exciting.
Margery started again, "But Mummy, why can't you come? They said you could!"
Agnes wiped away the hair that had fallen across Margery's eye.
"Girls, you know I can't leave Grandma, not on her own. Her arthritis is so bad now, how could she look after herself? Soon as you are settled I will come and visit. It will be much better for you living in the country. Then, as soon as the war is over, you can come straight home. Only a few more bits to pack, and then we will have a nice early tea, and a bath and hair wash. After all, you will want to look your best."

## When Life Changes Direction

Agnes could barely look at her five year old twins. Tomorrow morning, they were off somewhere safe. But when would she see them again? If only her Mother in law wasn't so frail. She dearly loved the old lady, but sending her daughters away like this was breaking her heart. Tommy, her husband, wasn't much help. He had arrived home on leave a few weeks ago, and said, as he wasn't around, it wasn't right for him to make the decision as to whether they stayed or were evacuated.

Tommy was a sailor in the navy, and had never been around much. Agnes often wondered if it would have been different if one of the girls had been a boy. She was sure he had said something along those lines to the Doctor the day after the girls were born.

It was an early start for the two little girls. Agnes woke the girls up at 4am. They slept end to end in a little bed in her bedroom when Tommy was at sea, but when he was on leave, their bed was moved in with their Grandma. It was a tight squeeze, but Tommy didn't really have much time for his twin daughters.

Margaret was out of bed, excited. This was a day of adventures. But when Margery opened her eyes, and saw the little cases in the corner of the bedroom, she immediately burst into tears. Agnes resisted going to her, as this day was going to be difficult for everyone.

By half past five, the two little girls were ready. Agnes, as a surprise for them, had made them a new blue dress and coat to travel in. Grandma had now made herself comfortable in the front room, and the two little girls ran to her to say goodbye. They dearly loved the old lady, and after she kissed them, and told them that for Mummy and Daddy's sake they must always be on their best behaviour, she pressed a shiny six penny piece in each of their right hands. Even Margery forgot her tears - a whole sixpence each!

Agnes carried the two small cases, and Margery clung to her right arm. Margaret was skipping along in front. They had nearly reached the school when Agnes called Margaret back,

"Girls, when you get to where you are going to, remember look after each other. You two are the lucky ones, no one else in your class is a twin, so you will we always have each other."

With that, she picked the two cases up, and they walked into the playground to line up with the rest of their class.

The buses were already at the school, and the children were counted onto them. It was like a military operation. The teachers left little time for the parents to say goodbye. Each child had their name on a label, which was pinned on to their coat lapel, and a small, square, cardboard box, which contained their gas mask, and their sandwiches for lunch.

Margaret and Margery sat together with another girl from their class. Agnes tapped on the window, so that they could wave goodbye to her. The twins could barely see over the side of the bus to look out of the window. With a jolt, the bus was off and the Mothers were running alongside trying to keep up, delaying the moment their children would be out of sight.

When Life Changes Direction


To Margaret and Margery, the bus ride didn't seem to take very long. Margery had been crying some of the journey, and the rest of the time they were trying to find her handkerchief, which had worked its way up the sleeve of her cardigan.

A stream of buses was pulling into Euston station. The children were told to collect all their belongings and line up in two's. By now, Margaret was getting bored by Margery's helplessness. She felt sad too in leaving her Mother and Grandma, but crying wasn't going to change anything. For a split second, she contemplated lining up with Dorothy, the little girl who had shared their seat, but this she knew would be wrong.

The twins had only ever been on a train once before, and were much younger, so had no memory of it. They were amazed to see how large the station was. It didn't take long to fill the train, and the two little girls found themselves in a carriage with their teacher. Even Margaret was pleased about this, as she was now feeling a little nervous of the train journey.

This part of the journey seemed to drag and, after a while, they were allowed to eat their sandwiches. Some of the smaller children fell asleep. The girls were used to sharing a bed and so, snuggled up to each other. They only awoke when the train pulled into it's destination.

Again they were told to collect their belongings, and get into two's, and the twins teacher, Miss Rogers, walked her class out of the station, across the road in to the church hall, of which they were the first to arrive at.

## Christine Friend

The children were shown where to leave their cases and where the toilets were. They were then instructed to take a drink and a biscuit off the table, and move to the other side of the hall. When the children looked behind, they could see other classes lining up to get into the hall - so there was no lingering.

After the girls had taken a drink and biscuit, they somehow managed to get split up. By now, groups of unknown adults were facing them. These were to be the 'Host Families'. It was at this point, that the children were being offered for billeting.

A very brusque, woman's voice could be heard speaking to the Vicar, and it sounded as if the Vicar was trying to placate her.

"Mrs Barnes, I am aware your husband is a church warden here, but it wouldn't seem appropriate for that to entitle you to be first to be allocated a child."

"I am sorry Vicar but I have a very clear idea of the type of child my husband and I would like to offer a home to. In fact, that little girl in the front row, with the beautifully made blue coat on."

With that, the Headmistress of the twins school stepped forward and took Margery by the hand and led her towards Mrs Barnes. But simultaneously, Miss Roger's noticed Margaret at the other end of the children and bought her forward.

Mrs Barnes was taken off her guard. She hadn't noticed that there was two children dressed exactly the same. She, never having had children of her own, was only prepared to take one child, and that was purely so she could be seen to be doing her bit. The reason she had chosen Margery was that she was by far, so much better dressed than the other children. The Vicar quickly made his way over, sensing that a situation was going to occur. By his side, was the billeting officer who was in charge of the operation. The look on Mrs Barnes face told everyone that she was not amused. Before she could say anything, the girls Headmistress stepped in.

"Hello, I am Miss Lee, Headmistress of Wykeham infant school in Stepney, where these two girls attend. They are twins, and therefore cannot be separated. So unless you are prepared to offer both a home, then I am afraid that they will have to be billeted elsewhere."

Mrs Barnes glanced across at the other children. At that particular moment, one of the boys was wiping his nose on his sleeve and none of the other little girls looked nearly as presentable.

She had been out manoeuvred, and reluctantly agreed to take both girls. The billeting officer beckoned her over to his table to complete the paperwork. The two sisters were instructed by their headmistress to collect their cases, and told that tomorrow or the following day, their class teacher would be paying them a visit. With that, they followed Mrs Barnes out of the church hall in view of more children waiting to be claimed.

What Margaret and Margery never noticed when they came out of the train station, was that they were surrounded by extremely nice houses. They followed Mrs Barnes, and she led them to a car which was parked just up from the Church. She tapped on the

window, and a man quickly got out of the driver's seat. She introduced him to the girls.
"Edward, this is Margaret and Margery. Girls, this is Mr Barnes, my husband. Now, if you would like to get in, Mr Barnes will put your things in the boot and we can go home."
If Edward Barnes seemed surprised to see two children, then he never let on to his wife. He dutifully put the cases in the boot, and then got back into the car and started the engine.
Today was certainly becoming a big adventure for the girls, as neither had ever ridden in a car before. They tried to look out of the window as they had on the train, but this time they were too small. In no time at all, the car had turned into a drive way. Mr and Mrs Barnes got out, and Mr Barnes saw to the cases. The little girls got out of the car - they had never seen such a large house. It was a new, 1935 detached brick built house, with a very large garden which wrapped itself around the house. They were later to discover that it had four bedrooms, and a bathroom upstairs.
The girls had had a very early start, and it was still only lunchtime. Mrs Barnes took them upstairs to show them the room in which they would sleep. It only had a single bed in it, but the twins could see it was bigger than their bed that they shared at home. Mrs Barnes was shocked when Margaret said,
"What a lovely bed Margery, which end are you going to sleep?"
In her normal, haughty voice, Mrs Barnes answered,

"You will only be sharing a bed until we can obtain another one. Now go to the bathroom and do the necessaries, and wash your hands and face, then come downstairs to lunch."
Mrs Barnes showed them to the bathroom. The girls were aghast. They had never seen a bathroom before. They were amazed at seeing a bath, no more bathing in the scullery in an old tin bath. Mrs Barnes told them not to be too long and then made her way downstairs. The twins looked at each other and said at the same time,
"What's the necessaries?"
Then, for the first time that day Margery giggled and said to her sister "It must mean go to the toilet."
The girls didn't hang around upstairs, they were used to being given orders and obeying them as this was how it was when Tommy, their Daddy, was home on leave.
At the bottom of the stairs, they could hear Mrs Barnes speaking and another lady answering. They looked at each other in surprise, was there a Grandma living in this house as well? They walked in the direction of the voices, and saw Mrs Barnes talking to a lady wearing a grey dress and white apron.
"Girls, come here."
Mrs Barnes was in the dining room and called them in.
"Margaret, Margery, this is Edna. Say 'hello'."
In unison, they said,
"Hello Edna."
Mrs Barnes continued.

"Edna works for Mr Barnes and me. She helps with all the household chores."
With the introductions over, the girls were shown where to sit.
Edna disappeared into the kitchen and returned carrying a large tray, with four plates of Shepherds pie on it. The plates were distributed, and Edna left the room. As soon as the door was closed, Mr Barnes Spoke.
"For what we are about to receive, may the Lord make us truly thankful, and keep us mindful of the needs of others, Amen."
The girls knew this happened at school but didn't realise that some people did this at home. For some reason, instinctively, they realised that putting their hands together and bowing their heads was the right thing to do.

After lunch, the girls were taken upstairs by Edna and were helped to unpack their belongings. After, they were told to take off their dress and cardigan, and to get under the top cover of the bed for an afternoon nap. Edna pulled the curtains across, and quite quickly they both fell asleep.

## *Chapter Three*

Back in Stepney, the house wasn't quite the same. Agnes found that from the moment she got back home after taking the girls to school, she just couldn't concentrate on anything. Old Mrs Bailey was upset at seeing the girls evacuated, and couldn't help feeling responsible for her daughter in law not going as well. She wasn't sure how to handle Agnes. Should she encourage her to have a good cry? Should she try and keep out of her way, or should she simply try and do all the housework that Agnes would normally do and show support? Mrs Bailey also wanted to ask where the girls were being sent to. Best put the kettle on and go from there.

Once the tea was brewed, Mrs Bailey called out to Agnes, who was upstairs. When she came down, it was clear she had been crying. Mrs Bailey got up from her chair and put her arms around her daughter in law, a strange concept for both of them.

While drinking their tea, Agnes told her Mother-in-law that the school would be letting them know on Monday morning where the children had gone to. As it was only Friday, it was going to be a long weekend. She was hoping that it wasn't too far, and that if the journey could be done there and back in a day, then there was every chance that she could go and visit them.

Agnes, other than shopping for the few bits that her and Mrs Bailey needed, spent Friday and Saturday working either in their small back garden, or dressmaking upstairs in her bedroom. There was only just enough room for a sewing machine and table in there. Agnes's dressmaking skills were in great demand, specialising in bridal and evening wear for the well to do. She was very meticulous and focused. As Agnes did all of her own cutting, there were always plenty of remnants of material. This enabled her to dress the twins in beautifully made clothes from expensive material but, she always felt it was such a shame they had to wear them with plimsolls, as shoes were simply far too expensive.

On Sunday morning, Agnes and Sarah stripped the Girls bed. It was while Agnes was at the copper in the scullery, and Mrs Bailey was sitting near her peeling potatoes, that they heard Neville Chamberlain announce that the Country was at war with Germany. While both women were coming to terms with the announcement, the siren rang out, warning of an air raid. Agnes helped Mrs Bailey get under the solid dining table. Neither of them could be believe that air raids were so imminent. Not long after, the all clear went. Poor Mrs Bailey, with help from Agnes struggled out from under the table. The thought of running to an air raid shelter seemed impossible, but the alternative of sheltering under the table didn't seem to be much better.

When Life Changes Direction

On Monday morning, Agnes made her way to the school. She acknowledged her neighbours on her way but didn't feel up to stopping for a chat. No one took offence. Agnes was a much respected member of the community. It was her husband Tommy that people didn't warm to. Everyone had their own problems, yet they admired how she looked after her Mother in Law and brought up her two little girls on her own. Tommy was never at home, he always seemed to be away on his ship.
Agnes made her way to the school office. The lists had been pinned to the wall. She found the list with her Daughters class number on it and read down it;

Margaret Bailey- St. Albans, Hertfordshire
Margery Bailey- St. Albans, Hertfordshire

The children's address would be received in the post, sent by the child or teacher. Obviously Agnes was concerned if the girls would be billeted together, but their teacher had assured her that they would be, so all she could do now was be patient, and wait for the letter.
The letter arrived two days later on the Wednesday morning. Agnes read with relief that both girls were being billeted together.

Christine Friend

*4<sup>th</sup> September 1939*

*Dear Mr and Mrs Bailey,*
*      Margaret and Margery have been placed in the care of Mr and Mrs Barnes. Both girls have settled well. I am hoping that in the not too distant future, some form of schooling will take place.*
*Their address is;*
*40 Larkswood Avenue*
*St.Albans*
*Hertfordshire*
*Mr and Mrs Bailey have stated that they would be happy for you to write to the girls.*

*Yours sincerely,*
*    Miss Rogers (Teacher)*


Agnes hurried into the front room to show her Mother in Law the letter. She read it aloud, as Mrs Bailey now had poor eyesight in one eye due to a cataract. They were both laughing with relief! Mrs Bailey asked Agnes to read out the address again, and remarked on how nice and middle class it sounded. Agnes agreed, and asked her if she would like to add something to her letter, which she was going to write that evening to her daughters.
Life carried on like that. Agnes wrote at least three times a week and would get the occasional postcard back from the girls. This she didn't mind. It was the

writing that was important. It made her feel close to them, after all, the girls were still only very young.

## *Chapter Four*

The week before Christmas Agnes had arranged for a neighbour to come and sit with her Mother in law so she could go and see the girls on a long awaited visit. On the morning of the visit, Agnes kept looking at the clock, and felt herself starting to panic. Unless the neighbour arrived soon she would miss her train. Mrs Bailey could sense her daughter-in-law's distress and urged her to leave. Agnes hesitated, but Mrs Bailey insisted she went.

It was a long journey, but Agnes didn't care, she was at long last going to see her darling daughters. She had plenty to carry, with two Christmas presents each for the girls, two new dresses and a winter coat each, gas mask and hand bag, she was laden down. During the journey, she thought about the new coats. She had managed to make them out of a large remnant of a very good quality green, heavy woollen cloth, the left over cloth being the benefits of her dressmaking skills. Making them in a duffle coat style with a hood, they would keep the girls lovely and warm during the coldest of winters. With forward thinking, she had also made the coats bigger than necessary so as to fit them the following winter.

 Eventually, she arrived at St. Albans station, and was met off the train by Mr Barnes. Agnes liked him immediately. Due to the shortage of petrol she did not have the luxury of a car ride unlike her daughters.

When Life Changes Direction

However, Mr. Barnes being the gentleman that he was, carried the clothes parcels for her. She was amazed when she saw the house. To think, her daughters were being bought up in such a lovely place. As quickly as she had warmed to Mr Barnes, she knew that Mrs Barnes was not a child friendly person. She hoped that Margaret, as the chatty one, had not discovered this for herself.

Agnes couldn't really see the girls when the front door was opened, as her eyes had welled up with tears. Mrs Barnes showed her into her front room and left her with her two excited daughters. The girls had so much to tell her. School was now three mornings a week in the church hall that they had been taken to on their arrival, and they planned to show her after she had had a hot drink, and warmed up. Then there was Edna, who Agnes had not yet met, who was a housemaid come cook. The girls were thrilled to tell Agnes about her. After lunch, Mrs Barnes had suggested they showed their Mother their bedroom. At this point Agnes could have cried with disappointment, thinking of her own home. Here, the girls shared their own room. It had two single beds next to each other, a dressing table and wardrobe, and a square carpet that covered most of the floor boards. They hung their new dresses and green duffle coats up with pride. Agnes was pleased she had made the clothes longer, as the girls had definitely grown.

It seemed no time before she had to leave. The twins held hands while they waved their Mother off, and at the same time, fought back the tears. Mr Barnes kindly walked her back to the station. It was now dark, and as there was no street lighting Agnes would have found it difficult to find her way back in such unfamiliar surroundings.

When they reached the station, she thanked him profusely for offering a home to her daughters. She made her way to the platform and waited for her train. By the time her train pulled in, Agnes was feeling absolutely drained, and very cold. It had been so lovely to see the girls, but so difficult to say goodbye again. She found a seat and fell into a deep sleep until the train pulled into Euston station. Back on the underground and then a bus ride. By now, she couldn't wait to be in her own home. It had been a long day. Eventually, she put her key in the front door and called out to her Mother in law. The blackout hadn't been pulled across the front door. She called out again, and could just hear her Mother in law's voice from the scullery. She dropped her bag and rushed in to find Mrs Bailey sitting on a chair, with her left hand wrapped in a tea towel. There was a smashed plate and food all over the tiled floor.

"Oh Mother what has happened... where is Mrs Jarvis, didn't she turn up?"

"Agnes I am so pleased to see you."

She started to get upset.

"It's OK, let me see your hand. We will sort that out first, and then you can tell my why you are here on your own."

When Life Changes Direction

Agnes dressed the cut, but first she put the kettle on. Mrs Bailey was in need of a hot drink.
Fortunately, the cut wasn't too deep. After it was dressed, Mrs Bailey explained,
"Mrs Jarvis just didn't turn up, so I heated up my dinner. It was as I tried to carry it to the table - my fingers just locked. I couldn't stop it smashing on the floor, and when I tried to pick up the pieces, one cut me. Agnes, I am so sorry. I have become such a burden to you, and today of all days! I so wanted you to come home to a warm house, it's the least you deserve after everything you do for me."
Agnes hadn't realised that the fire in the front room wasn't alight, and how cold it was. It was only then that she realised how bad the mess was on the floor. Taking her coat off, she went to the cupboard for the broom. Once the mess was swept up, she washed the floor with the remaining hot water from the kettle.
Mrs Bailey was starting to get upset again, realising how much work she had given her daughter in law.
Once the floor was clean, Agnes started looking through the cupboards wondering what she could give her Mother in Law to eat. She found a tin of soup, and cut some slices of bread.
It was only after they had finished their soup and bread, and drunk the tea, that Agnes told Mrs Bailey of her day.
She told the older lady of how well both the little girls looked, of the beautiful house that they were now living in, and of the maid that was in residence.

Christine Friend

The following day, there was a desperate knocking at the front door. Upon opening it, Agnes saw a very embarrassed Mrs Jarvis standing there.
"Agnes, I am so sorry to have let you down, but early yesterday morning my Ethel's waters broke and it isn't her time yet, three weeks early! I rushed round to hers, and left a note for our Johnny to bring over to you, but he never saw it and I only found out late last night when I got back home that you hadn't been told anything."
Eventually she stopped for breath and Agnes, feeling compassion towards her, invited her in for a cup of tea. Agnes and Mrs Bailey learned that Mrs Jarvis's first grandchild, a little boy, was delivered safe and well on the Saturday afternoon. After much reassurance from Mrs Jarvis that she wouldn't let her down again, she offered that at any time Agnes wanted to go to St.Albans, then she was to let her know.
Agnes promised that she would, and Mrs Jarvis went home feeling much relieved.

## *Chapter Five*

For Agnes to tell her Mother in Law her true feelings on visiting her daughters was something she couldn't contemplate. How could she tell Sarah how inadequate she felt as a parent. It wasn't only the material things the girls were now experiencing, but both girls glowed with the fresh air, and she was sure, a much better diet.
She felt she was losing her darling daughters, and was beginning to feel bereft. A feeling she had experienced before.

Back in 1916, Agnes's Mother died giving birth to her second child, this time, a little boy. Agnes had arrived home from school to see neighbours talking on the landing of their tiny tenement flat in Poplar. They didn't have much, her father was a docker working at West India dock. As soon as Agnes had been spotted, the talking turned into whispering. Agnes walked through the door to see her Father sitting at the table with his head in his hands. She thought he was crying, but, men *didn't* cry... did *they*? He called out to the neighbours on the landing, and Mrs Butler who lived next door took Agnes away into her home. It was there that Agnes was told her Mother and baby brother had both died.

Christine Friend

Agnes was six years old, and Instead of an adult stepping in and helping her with her grief, the roles reversed as her Father struggled to look after them both. When he was at work and there was no school, Agnes went into Mrs Butler's. She had four children, all younger than Agnes, and enjoyed having Agnes there to help, as she was a bright child, and good company. Agnes was a quick learner, and as time went on, her Father realised that she was more than capable, and grew to rely on her. She could prepare a stew mainly consisting of vegetables, and look after the range. By the time she left school, she was keeping a proper little home. Her school teacher, who could see a lot of potential in her, approached her Father wanting to know whether he would give his consent to her starting a dressmaking apprenticeship. This was the break Agnes needed.

She worked hard. Nothing was too much trouble and when one of the younger apprentices needed help, Agnes was always there. By the time her Father died when she was twenty two, she was an experienced seamstress. She wanted to leave Poplar. Her home life up until now wasn't particularly happy, and when mentioning this to one of her colleagues they told her of their Aunt who took in lodgers. Agnes went to see the Aunt, in Stepney. That was how Agnes met Tommy Bailey. He lived three doors away from where Agnes was lodging.

She, at the age of twenty two, had never had a boyfriend as there had always been too much to do at home. With Tommy's good looks and, seemingly cheerful disposition, she fell for him immediately. The fact that he was in the Navy didn't bother her, it would give her a chance to get to know his Mother, whose rented house they would live in once they were married.

Not only was Agnes not honest with Sarah, she wasn't completely honest with Margaret and Margery. Both Girls wanted to know how their Grandma was. She couldn't tell them of the incidents of incontinence she was having more and more frequently. Together with her arthritis, life had become very difficult for old Mrs Bailey.
Agnes had moved her Mother in Law's bed downstairs into the front room. The little bedroom had become her sewing room. This had made both of their lives easier. Mrs Bailey no longer had stairs to contend with, and Agnes could make good use of the extra room - now having some proper space to set up her cutting table to cut out the beautiful clothes that she made. Tommy would no doubt dislike the arrangement of his Mother sleeping downstairs, but his time on leave was always very short. Agnes still loved her husband, but she had grown to realise that Tommy Bailey was not the marrying kind.
 She had gradually seen more of the local children returning from their evacuated homes, but she knew as time went on she would never be able to cope. This way her little girls were safe and being well looked after. She had seen that for herself. There had been rumours of children not being looked after properly,

and being made to do manual work, but she felt blessed that her daughters were not billeted in one of those homes.

## *Chapter Six*

Margaret

The excitement of seeing her Mother had over taken Margaret's thoughts since the letter had arrived the week before from Agnes, giving the details of her visit. Mrs Barnes had read the letter out to them after breakfast, and Margaret immediately wanted to tell everyone she knew. She always felt that Mrs Barnes had the ability to spoil things, and this was no exception. However, when it was explained to her why she couldn't do this, she did understand . It would have been rather nasty to go and tell all her friends of the visit when most of them didn't even receive *letters* from their parents.

At five years old, Margaret was very aware of how people reacted to her. She had heard the altercation in the church hall the day they had arrived in St. Albans. She knew that Mrs Barnes only wanted one child, and that *she* wasn't that child. She couldn't say that Mrs Barnes didn't like her, because there wasn't anything to confirm this, but deep down Margaret knew she wasn't liked. In some ways, the attitude she received wasn't much different from that of her own Father, and she knew that would never change with him unless she could have become a boy.

Mr Barnes was different. He never really got to say anything and Margaret was sure he never made any decisions. He was a bank manager in the High Street, and therefore she knew he held a position of importance, but that wasn't the case at home. His hobby was jigsaw puzzles. Occasionally he would let the girls help him, but the pieces were very small and Margaret and Margery found it difficult to fit them in place without dislodging other pieces. He wasn't used to being around children so had very little conversation, nonetheless, the twins found him to be kind and generous to them.

Then there was Edna. She was really kind and seemed to understand how Margaret missed her Mother and Grandmother. Her life in Stepney may not have had the luxuries of an upstairs bathroom or her own bed, but a child needs affection, and here, there was little shown to Margaret. As the older twin she would try her hardest not to let Margery be aware of her homesickness.

A few weeks after the girls had moved in, Margaret was in the garden with her skipping rope. She was skipping away and singing the skipping song, 'Salt, Mustard, Vinegar, Pepper', when she heard a female voice call from the other side of the fence,

"I haven't heard that song in ages! It was one of my favourites when I was a little girl."

With that, a very tall, slim, extremely well dressed lady appeared above the fence. She was wearing her hair wrapped in a bright red turban, with rust coloured trousers and buttoned up cardigan. Her face was made up immaculately, with bright red lips. Margaret was mesmerised looking at someone so glamorous, and she couldn't believe they were actually talking to her. The lady introduced herself.

"Hello, I am sorry, did I startle you? My name is Penelope Waltham, and this is my house and my garden, which I love being in. Are you one of the evacuees living with the Mr and Mrs Barnes?"

Margaret couldn't stop herself from staring. The whole time this lady was speaking to her, she was smiling with her lovely red lips.

Margaret eventually found her tongue,

"Yes, my sister and I are twins, and my name is Margaret Bailey and my sister is called Margery. Our names aren't as pretty as yours".

Penelope laughed.

"That's so nice of you to say that. Yes I am lucky to have such a nice name, but Margaret is nice as well! After all, your name is the name of one of the royal princesses."

"Yes, that's what Mummy says."

With that, Margaret heard her name being called. She said goodbye to Penelope and went with her skipping rope back indoors.

It was Mrs Barnes calling. She wanted to know who Margaret was talking to, and pointed out that she should address the neighbour as 'Miss Waltham', and not use her first name.

Margaret was intrigued with Penelope, and hoped she would see her in the garden again quite soon.

That evening as Edna was helping the two little girls into bed, Margaret asked her about their next door neighbour.

Christine Friend

"Edna, who is the lady next door?"
"Who do you mean dear? One side is Mrs Green. She lives with her husband and two sons. One is now in the navy, and the other in the royal air force, so she might sometimes look a bit worried but she is a very nice lady. The other side is Miss Waltham. She is very nice as well, and I go every week to the cinema with Connie, her maid come cook, just like me".
"I met Miss Waltham today, while I was in the garden. She is ever so nice. She is like a film star."
Edna smiled,
"Yes, I suppose she does look like that, but don't let Mrs Barnes hear you talking about her. She doesn't think it the ladylike thing to do to go out to work. Although she seems to think it is OK for me! Miss Waltham owns and runs two very expensive dress shops, so she goes away a lot buying her stock."
Edna didn't really like saying this to Margaret, she was very fond of these two little girls, and she didn't want to see Margaret getting into trouble.
 Margaret loved seeing her neighbour in the garden, and from that day on, she would talk to her for as long as she could.

## *Chapter Seven*

Margery

Margery was born only five minutes after her sister, but enjoyed being called 'the baby' of the family. Margaret was always very protective of her. At times, their Mother treated her as a younger child. Margery didn't care. As long as there was someone to take care of them, then that suited her. So when their Mother came to visit, although Margery was very pleased to see her, she was a bit worried that her Mother would want to take them back home. At least half the children evacuated from their school had already been collected by their parents. This, she didn't want. This way of life was so much nicer. No more going out into the garden to use the privy, or 'lavatory' as they now called it. No more filling the coal scuttle up, and struggling to carry it indoors from the back garden with Margaret, so that their Mother could stoke up the fire. No more baths in the cold scullery. Now they bathed in a proper bath, with taps, and Edna would put a paraffin heater in the bathroom first! The thing Margery liked best, was having her own bed. She dearly loved her sister, but Margaret was a bit of a fidget, and often, when they shared, Margaret would wake her up.
Margery had very quickly got used to living in St.Albans with Mr and Mrs Barnes. She thought that Margaret

didn't particularly like Mrs Barnes. She didn't know why, but sometimes she would look at her sister and hope she wouldn't lose her temper and spoil things for them both.

It came as a relief to her when her mother explained to her and her sister that it was better that they stayed with Mr and Mrs Barnes. She told them that Grandma needed her help more and more, and that she was also working very hard so that she could send them little treats.

Margery had always thought that she had the prettiest Mummy but, today on her visit, she seemed to look different. Sadly, Agnes had aged in the short time the girls had been away. In fact, she was struggling not having her girls at home. The two things she had always hoped for when she had been a child, was a husband and children. She had achieved her goal but at the moment, she didn't live with any of them.

What surprised Margery was that Margaret had not mentioned her new friend to their Mother. Miss Waltham was nice, but Margery had overheard Mrs Barnes telling Edna that Miss Waltham was a bit fast. She had no idea what this meant, but as she was talking very quietly, she guessed it was something she shouldn't repeat. Anyway, Miss Waltham was away a lot, so it was much better to be in a house where there were adults to look after you and a routine everyday, even if it meant you did the same week after week.

Now that the girls had progressed with their reading, Mrs Barnes had registered them to the little library next door to their school. This was Margery's favourite thing; going to the library to return, and choose, a new book. She was making such good progress with her reading that Mrs Barnes had said that on their next visit, she could start borrowing two books at a time. She just always wished they could spend longer there choosing, but Margaret always managed to choose and exchange her book so quickly! The other thing that would worry Margery, was that the building had two purposes; three days a week, it would be used as a clinic for babies and children. Then, all of the equipment used would be put away in large cupboards, and the book shelves, which were covered over with sheeting, would be uncovered so that on the other three days it could be used as a library. The room in which the children's library was held had the biggest cupboard and, if left unlocked, Margaret would disappear inside and spend her time looking at things. Margery, being the quieter twin, would always worry that she would be caught and get into trouble. Fortunately for Margaret, that had never happened. She was far too aware how long it took for Mrs Barnes to change her books. With this in mind, she would always be standing at the entrance to the Children's room waiting for Margery to finish choosing when Mrs Barnes appeared.

## *Chapter Eight*

September 1940

The National and Local Newspapers all carried the same devastating story:

## *HEAVY BOMBING IN THE EAST END OF LONDON*

*At 4:56pm on the afternoon of Saturday 7$^{th}$ September 1940, air raid sirens wailed to alert Londoners of imminent danger. The German Air-force and the Luftwaffe launched a massive raid. By midnight, London's East End was engulfed in flames. The bombing lasted seven hours through the night.*

*490 London Civilians Dead*
*1,200 injured.*

The red glow in the sky was thought to be the sunset, but it was in the wrong direction... it was the reflection of the East End burning.

## *Chapter Nine*

Margaret and Margery

Very quickly, routines had been made in the Barnes household for the two little girls. Monday, Tuesday and Thursday mornings, there was school in the church hall. Mrs Barnes continued this theme for the rest of the day. Friday would be spent helping Edna with household chores, dusting and polishing, and any other little jobs that meant the house would be clean and tidy for any prospective visitors over the weekend. The little girls had real affection for Edna, they enjoyed their tasks, and being with her made them feel quite grown up.
The day the Girls would never forget, was Wednesday 11$^{th}$ September 1940. This was usually the girls favourite day of the week. In the morning, Mrs Barnes would take them into town, either to do a bit of shopping, which usually meant queuing (the twins didn't mind this) or, sometimes, they would go to the bank in the High Street, where Mr Barnes was the manager. When this happened, the staff were always very nice to them.
In the afternoon, Mrs Barnes would hand the girls over to Edna, and providing it was a nice day, then it would be a trip to the park. Margaret always skipped along in

front with her skipping rope while Margery walked behind holding Edna's hand.
This particular day, the weather was fine, and the girls had enjoyed their outing to the park. When they arrived back they heard Mrs Barnes calling them from the front room. The three of them looked at each other in surprise because, since the girls had been evacuated, the room had only been used three times; Christmas Day, Boxing Day and the day their Mother had visited. The twins realised this at the same time and hurriedly ran into the room hoping to see their Mother. But to their surprise, it was Mrs Barnes sitting with their teacher Miss Rogers.
Miss Rogers beckoned them to her. Margaret took hold of Margery's hand. When they were standing in front of her, she reached out and took hold of each little girls free hand, and then in a very quiet, and slow, precise voice, she spoke,
"Girls, you may have heard that, on Saturday, London was heavily bombed. A lot of people died. I am so sorry, but your Mother and Grandmother were caught up in the raids... they have both been killed."
Nobody spoke, the clock continued to tick, but no one moved. Tears were falling down the little girls faces, and then Margaret's voice cried out,
"No! Not our Mummy, it can't be true? Not our Mummy!"

## *Chapter Ten*

Sadly, that wasn't the only bad news to reach Larkswood Avenue that week. Mr & Mrs Green, next door neighbours to the Barnes', received the news that their son serving in the RAF's plane had crashed into the English Channel returning from a bombing raid in Germany, no survivors. It brought the war to the doorstep of those in St.Albans.

No one really knew how to treat the two little girls. The school had tried to find out if they had any other relatives other than their Father serving in the Navy. No one could provide any answers, and so Mrs Barnes contacted the authorities to say that, until their legal guardians could be found, she was happy to keep them. The authorities thanked her, and breathed a sigh of relief.

For Margaret and Margery, nothing changed in the few weeks after the devastating news. Then, at 9am on the Sunday morning, there was a knock at the front door. Mrs Barnes went to open the door, and to her surprise, it was Penelope Waltham standing there.

"Mrs Barnes, I am so sorry to bother you but, is it possible for me to have a private word with you?"

Mrs Barnes looked her up and down, 'didn't this woman realise we were at *war?*' Standing there all made up, with bright red lips and, to her critical eye, wearing a day dress that only she could dream of owning.

"Yes, please come in. Will it take long? As we will be leaving for church at about 9.30am. Mr Barnes has some duties to do before morning service."
"Ten, fifteen minutes may be?" Penelope replied.
Mrs Barnes showed her into the front room, saved for special occasions.
"I have been away for the last three weeks sourcing stock and materials for my shop and customers and, yesterday evening, upon my return, Connie told me the devastating news that Margaret and Margery's Mother and Grandmother had been killed in an air raid. I realise my experience with children is very limited, but I do know how it feels to lose your family at such a young age. My parents were both passengers on a night train travelling from Carlisle to St. Pancras station. The train had had to stop, and the following train ran into the back of the $1^{st}$ class sleeping car. My parents were both killed. It happened on the $2^{nd}$ of September 1913. I was thirteen. Then, a few years later when I had eventually come to terms with the loss, my brother was killed in the Somme. I just wanted to say that, if at any time you feel they may need a change of surroundings, I don't know, or someone else to talk to, then please think of me."
Mrs Barnes was taken aback with Penelope's revelations. She had never really spoken to her before, only to pass the time of day.
Penelope continued,
"I realise in the past I have spent a lot of time away, but part of my business is about having to change with the times, and I am diversifying into making female

uniforms for the elite. As such, I will be commuting every day to my business."

Mrs Barnes smiled, she knew that Margaret in particular, liked Penelope. She couldn't put her finger on it, but in many ways Margaret seemed so mature for her age, and had the habit of intensely looking at you which made you feel that she was disagreeing with you. Yet Margery was completely different type of child, lovely and easy going. So strange, when thinking that they are identical twins.

Mrs Barnes answered.

"That is extremely generous of you. I am sure that the girls would benefit from your experience of such tragedies. Perhaps if you are to be around sometime next weekend, the girls could spend some time with you? It would serve to break the routine. I am sure it would help".

Penelope wasn't sure if Mrs Barnes was trying to behave in a superior manner, but it didn't matter. She had enjoyed her chats with Margaret over the garden fence, and she was sad to think of her suffering now. Penelope thought best to make an arrangement now, that way she wouldn't have to knock again.

"Mrs Barnes, would it suit you if the girls were to come to tea next Sunday afternoon at 3pm and then I will bring them back at 6pm?"

"That sounds perfect, I will let them know. It will give them something to look forward to."

Mrs Barnes looked at her watch. Penelope took the hint.

## *Chapter Eleven*

At 3pm on the dot, Penelope knocked at 40 Larks wood Avenue. The twins were ready and waiting in the hall. Margaret was more enthusiastic than Margery, but up until now Margery had only seen Penelope from afar, whereas Margaret had chatted over the garden fence with Penelope on a few occasions now.

Mrs Barnes came and opened the front door. She was pleased to see Miss Waltham standing there, wearing a dress, and cardigan. She had heard that at weekends Miss Waltham was seen wearing trousers. This, she did not approve of, and the fact that it was a Sunday would have been even more inappropriate. The girls said goodbye, and as they walked down the drive, Mrs Barnes noticed Margaret take hold of Miss Waltham's hand. She still felt a slight coldness to the little girl, but nonetheless, she was a little disappointed after seeing this, as Margaret had never done that with her.

The girls couldn't believe how different inside Penelope's house was to that of the Barnes'. All of the inside paintwork was a brilliant white. There was a flowery smell all around, this was matched by the soft furnishings which all had a flowery pattern, or as Penelope called it, "chintzy".

She showed them into her front room, and said that they had three hours, and she wanted them to enjoy every minute - so they needed to plan their afternoon. The girls thought the sound of this was very exciting.

When Life Changes Direction


Whilst they were deciding, Margaret couldn't stop looking at the large photo on the wall above the sideboard. It was a photograph of a young and beautiful woman and a young gentleman. Margaret knew by the woman's dress that it was a wedding photo, as she had seen many wedding dresses being made by her Mother - but who were they? Penelope noticed her looking,
"Isn't it a lovely photograph. It is my parents on their wedding day."
Margaret was totally enthralled and asked,
"Where are they now? Do they live in St.Albans?"
Penelope's smile faded, and for the first time Margaret saw a look of sadness.
"No, they were killed in a train crash, quite a long time ago now. I was thirteen, older than you but still far too young to lose my parents."
Penelope now had both girls full attention, so she continued.
"They were travelling from Carlisle to St. Pancras station in London.
I had an older brother - Hugh - but he wasn't married then, so after the crash I carried on at my boarding school, and then on school holidays I would go to my Grandmother's."
Penelope looked at their little faces. The talk of death was far too soon after their own tragedy, she had to lighten the mood.
"How would you both like to have tea in the garden? The afternoon is still warm, and before tea I can show you all the hard work I have done - which I am actually

very proud of! First we must let Connie know that we are going to eat outside."
Margery asked if that meant a picnic.
"Well I suppose it is a kind of picnic except, that it is on a table. Come on, I'll show you."
The girls loved the inside of her house, but they were amazed at the garden. Mr and Mrs Barnes had put a trellis all along the top of the fence, and with the plants that grew on it, it blocked any view of Penelope's garden.
By the back of Penelope's house there was a glass roof extending out, and under the roof was a wooden table and chairs and chintzy cushions. The other side of the roof was a wooden structure that was covered by a grape vine. Once you had walked through this area, the garden opened out. There was a huge lawn with flower beds down each side and dotted around in the lawn were six small beds, all planted with rose trees. Once the three of them had walked past these, they came to a sunken garden with steps down, and up and the other side, and there was a little orchard of five fruit trees.
The girls found it so interesting, and Penelope was clearly pleased with the reaction from them.
After they had eaten their tea in the garden, Penelope suggested that they went indoors and played a game. The previous week she had made a trip to Hamley's the toy shop in Regent Street. The assistants were most helpful, and she bought the recommended games of snakes and ladders, playing cards, and ludo. It was only when she got home and was showing Connie

what she had bought, that Connie pointed out that Mrs Barnes might not like the girls playing cards - especially on a Sunday.

Fortunately, the girls chose to play snakes and ladders. They played two games, with Margery winning both. By now it was almost 6pm.

Agnes had always instilled good manners, and when it was time to leave, the little girls went and thanked Connie for their lovely tea.

Skipping in front of Penelope, the girls were soon back to the Barnes' house. Mrs Barnes answered the door and the girls thanked Miss Waltham.

Penelope didn't want to appear too pushy by asking Mrs Barnes if they could come to tea the following Sunday, but she needn't have worried. Mrs Barnes on saying goodnight, suggested the same arrangement. This began a new routine, Sunday afternoon at Miss Waltham's.

# *Chapter Twelve*

Penelope

I could have cried when Margaret asked where my parents were. Perhaps I should have removed my parents wedding photo. At least until the twins had got to know me a bit better. Looking back, grief is a terrible thing, and at least the subject had been bought out into the open. Hiding terrible news helps no one, I should know.

When my boarding school received the news that both of my parents had been killed in the train crash, I was immediately packed off to my Grandmother's, where she dispassionately broke the tragic news. Why I wasn't told at school I don't know, not even to this day. Her house was like a mausoleum. It was cold, even in the summer. When I arrived, it was a sunny September day. The house keeper met me at the front door and showed me into my Grandmother's sitting room. The fire was alight, and it made the room very hot and clammy. My Grandmother beckoned me to her. In a very clear voice, she informed me that I would have to temporarily live with her and my Grandfather. They didn't like noise or disobedient children. That was funny because I never thought my Grandmother liked any kind of children!

After that brief meeting, I rarely saw either of my Grandparents. They lived by the saying, 'Children should be seen, not heard', but in this instance they didn't seem to like seeing me either.

Fortunately for me, I had always enjoyed my boarding school, and I made many good friends. Sometimes during a school holiday, I would be invited to stay at a friend's, house which was heaven. Although I was never given the opportunity to reciprocate the invitation, in some ways I was relieved, as staying at my grandparents could never be considered as fun.

When I was seventeen and only had a couple of months left at school, my Grandfather died. Having outlived his only child - my Father - and my brother having been killed in the Great War, he left everything to my Grandmother.

Life changed quite dramatically after that. My Grandmother had always accused my Grandfather of being mean, and although she didn't particularly like me, she disliked my Grandfather even more. Our lifestyle became more extravagant and I was given a very healthy allowance, something my Grandfather would certainly not have approved of. After leaving school, I filled my days by being tutored at home; French, sewing, and art lessons. Grandmother had also started to entertain a lot, and with my help, we had some most interesting, and enjoyable evenings. How much longer this lifestyle would have carried on I don't know, I suppose at some point Grandmother would have had to have found me a suitable husband, but it never came to that. On the day of my twenty first Birthday she asked me what I would like to do with my

life - she was not a fool and would have known if I had made something up to please her - and so I told her, "Grandmother, I would like to open my own ladies clothes shop; Buying from small, elite companies, that could offer style, class ,and from day to evening wear - but not at couture prices."
To my shock, she immediately agreed to the idea and wanted to finance the whole venture! There was to be one condition. Quite simply, her Solicitor had to oversee all of my plans. The deal was struck, and I never looked back.

## *Chapter Thirteen*

For the next eighteen months, the girls routines changed very little other than their place of schooling. There were only a handful of evacuees left in St. Albans from the twins school in Stepney. With so few children, it was easy to incorporate them in to the local junior school. Therefore the church hall was no longer used. Miss Rogers - the girls first teacher - had also remained. She had been lucky enough to take the place of a male teacher, who had been called up.
It was March 1942, and the twins were now eight years old. It was a Tuesday morning, and a school day. As they were coming down the stairs, the postman was dropping two letters through the letter box, on to the floor. They picked up one each and Margaret looked at hers. To her delight it was addressed ;

Margaret and Margery Bailey
40 Larkswood Avenue
St.Albans
Hertfordshire

The girls were delighted - they hadn't received any letters since their Mother had died. They gave the post to Mrs Barnes, but she said they were old enough to read their own post. Margery opened the envelope and passed the letter to Margaret to read out loud.

Both the girls were good readers, but Margery still liked to think of herself as the baby. Margaret read;

*'Dear Maggie and Marg,*

*I am home on leave and coming to see you on Thursday,*

*From your Dad'*

Mrs Barnes was taken aback. The girls had now been living with her and Mr Barnes for two and half years, and this was the first time their Father had made any sign of contact. Not even after his wife and Mother had been killed had he sought to contact his daughters. For the Girls, it was a mixture of excitement and weariness. It had been so long since they had heard from him or seen him. That in all honesty, they never gave him a second thought. Although neither of them mentioned it to each other, they were both worried that he intended to take them away.

Mrs Barnes voiced this same concern to her husband. Mr Barnes tried to reassure her that, in his considered opinion, if he had any plans to do so then he would have been in contact much sooner.

The next two days seemed like an eternity for Mrs Barnes. She had written to the girls' teacher explaining that, due to their Father's shore leave, they would be absent from school on the Thursday. She also made arrangements with Edna so as to be able to offer dinner and tea to the girls' father, as in his letter, he gave no indication of time, or length of stay.

On Thursday morning the girls were up early. The excitement for Margaret had started to wear off. She had started to remember her Father's indifference to her, but she was also concerned about leaving, and never seeing Penelope again.

Margery just felt tearful. Mr and Mrs Barnes house was home for her now. She didn't want to leave, she had got used to her comfortable life.

The girls were sitting in the front room reading when there was a knock at the front door. Mrs Barnes got up from her armchair and answered it. The girls could hear the exchange of words, and although they couldn't hear what was being said, they knew their Father had arrived as they could clearly hear his voice. Mrs Barnes showed him into the front room. It was over three years since they had last seen him.

Margaret and Margery thought their Father looked much the same, but Tommy was surprised at how much the girls had grown. In front of him stood two tall, eight year old girls, they had their Mother's good looks and beautiful brown curly hair.

"Come on girls, give your old Dad a kiss!"

The girls ventured forward holding hands, which they did when they wanted reassurance from each other. They both gave him a kiss on the cheek. Mrs Barnes asked him if he would like a cup of tea.

"Yes, a cuppa would be most welcome. Now girls, how are you getting on at school? Good, I hope. Come and tell me everything."
Mrs Barnes withdrew to the kitchen. As soon as the kitchen door was closed, Edna's curiosity was too much.
"So Mrs Barnes, what is he like? Their mum was such a nice lady."
"If you must know Edna, he is common. I grant you, I can see how Mrs Bailey fell for him as he has good looks, and a certain rough charm, but she was a very nice person, and I am sure she could have done better."
That said it all. Edna got on with preparing the lunch and started to say a little prayer to herself, hoping that his visit was not about taking the girls away.
As it turned out, all the worrying had been totally unnecessary. When Mrs Barnes had left the room, Tommy had a good look around.
"Well girls, landed on your feet here! Has the old tartar any children?"
Margaret answered - Margery had become a bit shy.
"No children, it is just Mr Barnes, Edna their sort of maid, and us."
Tommy raised an eyebrow.
"Well girls, a word of advice. You are on to a good thing living here. If they have no kids, then one day this could all be yours."
He had just finished speaking when Mrs Barnes came in with a tray laden with tea things. She poured the tea and handed a cup to Tommy. He drank it straight

down, looked at the clock on the mantelpiece, and said,

"Right girls, time I was off... going back to my ship tonight."

He gave their heads a rub, took his sailor's cap out of his pocket, and put it on. Then he went into the hall where the girls could see he had left his sea bag, he picked it up, gave the girls a wave and was gone. Margaret wasn't sure who was more surprised; Mrs Barnes, or them. It was over. He had no intention of taking them away. Margaret and Margery were to remember this day for the rest of their lives.

Mrs Barnes breathed out a sigh of relief. Margery was here to stay. In the short time he had spent with them, he had made no mention of money or a contact address. This surpassed all of Mrs Barnes dreams.

Later that week, she was to find out from one of her neighbours that a young girl had been standing on the corner of their road smoking at the same time Tommy Bailey was visiting, and both had been seen later getting on a train, bound for London.

# *Chapter Fourteen*

Margaret and Margery knew that, from now on, 40 Larkswood Avenue was their home. In some ways they had listened to their Father, as both worked as hard as they could at school and both had been recommended to sit the eleven plus. By passing this exam, it would lead them to a place at the local grammar school for girls. Mrs Barnes attitude to the Girls beginnings didn't change. She felt she had brought the girls on a long way from their birth place in Stepney.

Summer 1945 was to be a time of celebration in the Barnes household, and not only because the Second World War was finally over, freedom and peace at last, but Margaret and Margery had both passed the eleven plus. In September they would be taking their places in St. Albans Grammar school for girls.

They both proved to be hard working in their new school. Their talents lay in different areas. Margaret showed a talent for mathematics and grasped many mathematical concepts very quickly. Margery favoured English. She was slower when it came to anything tactical, and that included sports, but she was happy to spend time on her own and study.

A few weeks after the war had ended, Mrs Barnes contacted the Authorities regarding her two evacuees. Other than Margaret, Margery and their former teacher Miss Rogers, all the other evacuees and staff had returned to their homes in Stepney.

As far as her husband and she were concerned, the girls had no relatives other than their errant Father. As Tom Bailey had been serving in the Royal Navy, they had no idea as to whether he had even survived the war. Their problem was, if he had, would he want to take the girls away? Mr and Mrs Barnes were both unhappy at the prospect of this happening. Margaret and Margery had nearly spent as much of their lives with the Barnes' as they had in Stepney. If you took into account the girls baby years, then most of their memories were in St. Albans.

Mr and Mrs Barnes biggest concern was that they had no legal rights, and were worried for the girls. They decided that the best thing to do would be to contact the local authorities. Mrs Barnes was not one to be intimidated by formality, in fact she quite enjoyed the challenge.

As it happened, Mr and Mrs Barnes were worried unnecessarily. They were informed that, unless they were going to move from the area – making it difficult for their Father to find them – there was no issue with the girls remaining in their care. The local authorities were more concerned that the Barnes' had wanted to relinquish their duties as they had plenty of emergency cases to deal with, and were relieved the twins' case was not added to their workload.

However, there was something said that made Mrs Barnes think. She was asked what the girls called her and her husband. When she asked why, it was pointed out that by being called by their prefix and surname, it made it a very formal environment for the girls to live in. Obviously Mother and Father wasn't appropriate, but had she considered letting the girls call them 'Aunt' and 'Uncle'? This way they would be providing a home for the girls with more of a *family* connotation. Mrs Barnes could see the sense in this.

The following Sunday after breakfast, Mr and Mrs Barnes decided that this would be the best time to explain the change to the girls. Margery readily agreed and thanked Aunt Edith and Uncle Edward. Margaret had never felt particularly close to either of them, but did with Miss Waltham and seized on this opportunity to suggest calling her 'Aunt Penelope'. She had trumped Mrs Barnes, and of course Mrs Barnes had no choice but to agree. Margaret noticed the sharp look Aunt Edith gave her, but she didn't really mind, especially as she had no intention of calling Miss Waltham, 'Aunt'. It would be, 'Penelope'.

The girls received a lot of encouragement at school, and received a heavy amount of homework. Margery would use this as an excuse to stop visiting Penelope on a Sunday afternoon. It wasn't that she didn't like Penelope, it was more that she had to make an effort to join in. Whereas at home, she could disappear up to the bedroom and read to her hearts content. At the beginning, Margaret missed her sister and felt embarrassed when she had to explain that she was on her own, but as time went on, she and Penelope had so much to say to each other, that she got used to it.

## When Life Changes Direction

In no time, the girls were going to be turning sixteen. Their birthday was in January. It was early November on a Monday morning, and Aunt Edith opened the front door to find Penelope standing there.
"Good morning Mrs Barnes, have you a few moments? I have been thinking about the girls' future and, well, I wanted to discuss a possible idea with you."
"Please come in. It is rather cold out there today."
She led Penelope into the front room, and both ladies sat down. Penelope had been rehearsing this speech for a couple of days. She didn't want to appear too pushy, after all the girls were not really anything to do with her, but this would be perfect for Margaret. Penelope began;
"I am not sure how much Margaret has told you about my business? Now that the war is over, and Christian Dior has bought out the New Look, small businesses like my own are doing very well. I have two shops in the West end, but in the next couple of years I would like to open another shop, perhaps in a different type of location... I am sorry if I am prevaricating but I thought a little background knowledge would make clear my idea. So, with this in mind, and the fact that I will still need to go to shows and see manufacturers, if I was to take on a trainee then - when trained - they could deputise for me. They would be taught all aspects of the business, it would be an excellent career for the right person."
Mrs Barnes looked very thoughtful, and then she spoke,

"And you think that person would be Margery?"
Penelope's heart missed a beat,
"No, actually I was thinking of Margaret. From what I gather from the girls, Margaret is very good at mathematics, and the opportunity I am offering would require her to do a day release course in book keeping. Margery, when we have talked about what she would like to do as a career, has always made me think that she would like to work locally, possibly in a library?"
Mrs Barnes was now staring at Penelope, and Penelope was beginning to think that she had said too much! Then, all of a sudden, Mrs Barnes face broke in to a full smile. Something Penelope had never seen before. In fact, Penelope thought it a shame that she didn't smile more often, as it completely changed her haughty looking face, and actually made her quite an attractive woman.
"Miss Waltham, of course I would have to discuss your idea with Mr Barnes, and also both of the girls. We wouldn't want Margery to feel left out, but I understand what you mean about Margery, she is far more of a sensitive, homely girl."
Penelope agreed with her, although secretly she thought Margery was a little lazy.

The following Sunday, Margaret could not wait for her weekly visit to her next door neighbour. Margery had decided that she would rather finish the book she was reading. It was going to take a bit more than a game of cards and a nice tea to get her away from reading in front of the fire.

When Life Changes Direction

At 3pm, Margaret was knocking at Penelope's door, and was already taking her coat off when Connie came to answer,
"Hello Connie, where is Penelope I have got some great news!"
Connie had already been told by Miss Waltham of her visit to the Barnes' household.
"Come in, and hang your coat up. She is upstairs, but won't be long. Come into the front room, it is lovely and warm."
For Margaret, it seemed that she was waiting for ages, but actually within minutes Penelope, was entering the room. Margaret immediately started to speak,
"We had a family conference, that's what Aunt Edith called it last night. Is it really true that you have offered me a job as a trainee? Because if it is, I accept! And Aunt Edith and Uncle Edward both think it is a really good opportunity for me, and are also happy for me to accept."
"That's excellent news Margaret, but how did Margery take it?"
"She was actually relieved. To start with, Aunt Edith didn't let on who the job was for, and I was praying it was me - and Margery was praying it wasn't her! It's funny, but Aunt Edith said that you thought Margery would enjoy working locally in a library, and when she said this, Margery said that would be her perfect job. How did you know?"
"Oh, I suppose in my line of business, I look at my clients and try and analyse them. Do they go to work? If they do, what do they do for a living? Can they

choose what they like to wear, or do they have to please their husband? How much money do they have to spend?"
They both were now laughing.
"I see, and that is one of the things you are going to teach me as a trainee?"
"One of the things - yes - but I think for you - as it did with me - it will come naturally. All I am going to ask, is that you carry on working hard at school and get your qualifications."
Margaret readily agreed.
There were no games of cards that afternoon. For the rest of the visit, Penelope outlined her plans. Margaret listened intently. She couldn't help thinking of her Mother, she was sure Agnes would be proud to think that her daughter would be advising the upper classes on how to dress in the sort of clothes that Agnes had once made.

Now Margaret's future was settled, Aunt Edith took control of Margery's. There were three libraries in St. Albans. The library/ clinic that Mrs Barnes took the twins to during the war, closed soon after the war had ended. The main busy library was in the High Street, not far from Uncle Edward's bank. The Chief librarian frequently went into his bank, and was known on a professional basis by Uncle Edward. Once this had been revealed to his wife, Edward was instructed to make enquires on any vacancies in the near future that would suit Margery.

When Life Changes Direction


As luck would have it, a vacancy would open up the following July. One of the smaller libraries had a female member of staff, who was leaving to get married. The Chief librarian understood that Margery might like a few weeks holiday after leaving school, but if she was to come and see him - and there was no hurry - then he would hold the job for her. Aunt Edith couldn't be more pleased.

During the Easter school holiday, Penelope had asked Mrs Barnes if she might take both girls up to town for the day. In the morning, she would show them both where Margaret was to work, have some lunch, and then perhaps go to one of the museums. The Victoria and Albert museum, she thought, would be a good choice. Something of interest for both the girls.
The day was a big success, and Penelope treated both the girls to a suit from her shop. For Margaret, it was a good investment - she would need it for work. Penelope wouldn't dream of treating the girls differently, and the suit would be something for Margery to wear for her forthcoming interview.

Margery, who had always been indifferent to clothes, actually enjoyed wearing her suit, and felt it gave her a lot of confidence when she had her interview with the Chief librarian. He in turn, was impressed with her. He had never met a sixteen year old with such a wide knowledge of literature as Margery. She literally just loved reading, and had read; all the classics, a wide range of popular novels, biographies, and, knew her way around a reference book. He was so impressed that he thought she would be wasted at the smaller library, so he decided that she should be employed in the main library. Margery was thrilled. That meant that four days out of every week, she could travel to work with Uncle Edward in his car.

The girls last day at school was Friday 21st July. They were going to have a family holiday in Southwold for a week, staying in a guest house. The girls were excited. It was to be their first holiday ever, and then home for one week organising themselves, before starting work on Monday $14^{th}$ August.
The week before their holiday, the twins exam results arrived. As forecasted, both girls did extremely well. Margaret had excelled in mathematics, and Margery in English language and literature.

## *Chapter Fifteen*

Margaret was absolutely captivated by her new job. She excelled in every aspect. She seemed to know which customers would warm to such a young assistant and those who thought her too inexperienced. Alterations were done on the premises by Ada, the seamstress, who had her own little sewing room. If Margaret ever had a spare minute, then this is where she would be. She always found it so comforting listening to the sewing machine, it reminded her of her early childhood. The rest of the staff realised she was Penelope's protégée, but no one minded. At some time in the future they knew she would become the deputy manageress, but she fitted in so well and was such a hard worker, that everybody liked her. Penelope began to think of her as much more than a neighbour, or even a friend, and saw her as the daughter she would never have.

Margery also did well. She liked the quiet, and unhurried manner in which the library worked. Most of the borrowers were nice people. In the reference library, that days newspapers were delivered. Margery, when working in that department, got to know the regulars, and would try and have a glance through the newspapers before the library opened so as to direct them to the pages they would most enjoy.

Christine Friend

Neither of the girls was yet to have a boyfriend – much to the delight of Mrs Barnes. It was surprising, as both girls were real beauties, and had grown to mirror their Mother, including her thick, shiny hair. Margery was basically quite shy with young men. Margaret wasn't, she just didn't want any distractions. She wanted to prove to herself that she could excel in her career. She also felt she owed Penelope a huge debt of gratitude, due to the trust and belief that had been shown in her. She certainly didn't want to end up like her Mother, whom she adored, but recognised the hard life she had had by marrying Tommy Bailey.

Margery would travel to work with Uncle Edward four days a week, then on a Saturday it would be by bus. It was a twenty minute ride, but as always when Margery had free time, she had her head in a book. On a Saturday, she would go to the cinema with her Aunt, and sometimes with her Uncle as well. Occasionally, they would be joined by Margaret - but only if she managed to get home on time.

Margery always had a day off in the week, and would often spend it writing reviews for the borrowers at the library. At school, she had made friends with another quiet girl, Daphne. Daphne had started work in the accounts department in Harris's, the main store in the High Street. At least once a month, the two girls' day off would coincide, and they would meet up.

If Margaret went to college one day a week, then she was entitled to another day off to make up for her working Saturdays. Margaret tried to explain to Margery however, that if she took another day, as well as Sunday and her college day, then she would only be in the shop for four days a week. Margery wanted her to take the extra day so that she would have some company, but Margaret was far too focused for that.

Margaret's college course of book keeping and general office practise was going very well. It was giving her the background knowledge of how to run a business effectively. Her tutor at the college was surprised by her maturity, and could see that she was she would go far, working as hard as she did.

In May 1952, Margaret's two year course was nearly at an end. Penelope could see how good she was with figures, and wondered if working in her business was really the right vocation for her.
Penelope decided to speak to Margaret about this out of the confines of her business premises, so travelling home one evening in an unusually empty train carriage, she raised the question,
"When I started out, Margaret, owning and running my own business was all I wanted to do. I think I have realised my limitations, and I have fulfilled my ambition - I am not so sure I judged your limitations as accurately. Your college report is glowing, especially the book keeping side."
Penelope looked directly at Margaret, and instantly realised that Margaret was worried about what she was going to say next.
"Margaret, there is nothing to worry about. Your job is there for you regardless, but, I did wonder if you would

find it fulfilling enough? And if not, would you let me sponsor you for further education, perhaps university?"

Margaret's face broke into an immense smile. "Penelope, I thought for a minute that you had changed your mind and no longer wanted me to work for you! I am so happy working for you, and my ambition is to become one of your deputy managers. I love working in the clothes industry. It makes me feel close to my Mother. I know that what she used to do is so totally out of my league, but I do think that, with my head for figures and knack for sales, that this is where my future would be."

"Of course there is no doubting your talent for dressing our customers, and yes I can see you in a management role, but if at anytime you should change your mind then all I ask is that you come and tell me. I don't want you to feel unhappy, or that you are being ungrateful in any way."

With Penelope's question answered in the most emphatic way, she sat back in her seat feeling very satisfied.

## *Chapter Sixteen*

Something Penelope had always considered doing, was having a 'busman's holiday'. She had wanted to travel to Paris and Milan, and see the big fashion houses at work. She had contacts, so she was sure she would have plenty to see - and a two week vacation would do her good. Other than weekends away, and business trips lasting two to three days, she had not left her business for a number of years. Penelope had plenty of friends, male and female, but if she was to take this trip with someone, she wanted it to be someone who would benefit from it. It was obvious that the only person it could be was Margaret. Even though she had worked for her for two years, when it came to birthdays and Christmas, Penelope treated the twins in the same way. That meant that they were always given the same present.

Therefore, the following Wednesday morning when she knew Margaret was at her South Kensington shop, and Margery would be at the library, Penelope knocked at 40 Larkswood Avenue. Mrs Barnes had seen her out of the bedroom window walking up her drive, and was preparing herself for the next favour.

"Good morning Miss Waltham, please come in. Edna was just about to make coffee, please, come and join me."

If Mrs Barnes was hoping to take Penelope off guard, then she succeeded. Penelope smiled sweetly and readily agreed. She had already planned to have her morning coffee sitting out in her own garden on this warm, bright, sunny, May day, but if this was the means to an end then, well, 'hey ho'.

Once both ladies were sitting in the front room, and Mrs Barnes had poured the coffee, Penelope started to set out her intended plans.

"Mrs Barnes, I am sure you will agree that, both the girls have worked inordinately hard since starting their chosen career paths. In September, I am planning for myself a long awaited trip to France and Italy, staying a week in each. If you and Mr Barnes are happy for me to, I would like to take the twins with me. Margaret would benefit greatly in dealing with clients. They often want to talk about their travelling experiences, and it would benefit Margaret if she had some experience herself. I think it would also be beneficial to Margery in her role on the desk, in the reference library. All travelling is a good experience."

She came to an abrupt end, feeling that she was trying too hard to sell the whole idea.

Mrs Barnes looked directly at her, giving no indication as to whether the answer would be a 'yes' or a 'no', then replied,

"I see, that is a lot to think about. If you don't mind, I will discuss it with my husband first. After all, we wouldn't want to upset the girls if we didn't think it would work, but Miss Waltham it is a very generous offer, and I thank you on the girls behalf."

For the second time, she started to smile, and this Penelope found very unnerving. Fortunately, by now she had finished her coffee, so she complimented Mrs Barnes on how lovely her garden looked, and bid her good morning.

It wasn't until the Saturday morning, that Penelope noticed how Margaret wasn't her usual, bubbly self. She *had* been dealing with one of their more exacting clients, but Penelope had always been pleased how Margaret never let them get to her. She didn't want this mood to escalate, so she asked Margaret to join her in the office, telling her there was something she needed to show her. It wasn't long before she told Penelope what was on her mind. It was Margery, she was adamant that she didn't want to travel, and go to France and Italy. Mr and Mrs Barnes had had one of their family conferences on the Friday evening. Margaret was upset at the thought of leaving her twin sister at home, but also worried that if Margery didn't go, then she wouldn't be allowed to go either. Penelope enquired how it was left,

"Well, Aunt Edith thinks that until Margery is one hundred per cent sure she doesn't want to go, then the options for me will have to wait. Margery can be so lazy sometimes it's only because she can't be bothered!"

Penelope did happen to agree with Margaret, but didn't voice this opinion. Instead, she said,

"Let's just forget about it, and focus on today's work. I am sure it will all work out for the best."

Whether it was to build a sense of drama, or just that Mrs Barnes didn't want to be beholden to Penelope,

but the holiday was not discussed again in the Barnes household until the following Friday evening at yet another family conference.
Margery was quite clear in that she didn't want to go abroad now, and possibly would never want to go. Margaret was sitting at the table with her arms folded and her fingers crossed. She had tried to talk Margery round during the week, but to no avail. Now Margaret was annoyed with her. The opportunity Penelope was offering them both was something they could only dream about.
Mrs Barnes held court.
"Margery, are you sure you want to turn Miss Waltham's offer down?"
Margery didn't hesitate,
"I won't change my mind. It's very kind of her but I know it isn't for me."
Then looking at Margaret, Margery added.
"Margaret, that doesn't mean you can't go. You will probably have more fun if I am not there anyway."
Margaret dared not answer. If Mrs Barnes knew how much she wanted to go, she would say no just because it was her. It became very quiet, and then Mr Barnes made a contribution to the conversation.
"Well it all seems very straight forward to me. Margaret can go on her own, then at least that way Miss Waltham won't think her generous offer is being snubbed and both girls get to make their own choice."
Mrs Barnes nodded in agreement and seemed to close the discussion by asking if anyone would like a hot drink.

## When Life Changes Direction

It wasn't until Margaret said goodnight that Mrs Barnes said with a smile on her face.
"Margaret, would you like to tell Miss Waltham tomorrow that you can accept her offer, and perhaps, Margery, it would be nice if you wrote her a little note."
Both girls agreed, and were happy with the suggestions. Margaret was so excited. Margery was just relieved that she wouldn't have to face Penelope and tell her she didn't want to go.

## *Chapter Seventeen*

The weeks leading up to Margaret's trip to France and Italy were very busy. She had become quite accomplished with a needle, and adapted some of her summer clothes from the previous year to make them a little more stylish. She hadn't any dresses suitable for the evening, so Penelope had allowed her to go through some old stock, and with the help of Ada the seamstress, altered these to fit perfectly. Penelope didn't want Margery to feel left out, so asked Ada to make a couple of new day dresses for both girls. Margery was very pleased with her new clothes as it would save her the bother of having to shop for them herself.

The big day arrived, and for Margaret it reminded her of the day that her and her sister were evacuated. It was an early start for both households as Aunt Edith, Uncle Edward and Margery, all waved the taxi off at 6 o'clock in the morning. Margaret hugged her sister close, and then, to her surprise, her Aunt and Uncle both kissed her goodbye. She didn't dwell on this unusual gesture until a few weeks later.

The flight was from London Airport to Paris. Margaret, never having flown before, wasn't sure whether to be scared or excited. But everything seemed to be happening so fast that her anxiety left her, and excitement took over.

## When Life Changes Direction

For Penelope and Margaret, the first week flew by. There was so much to see and Margaret bought postcards of all the sights they visited to keep as souvenirs. It wasn't all sightseeing, shopping was high on the list as well, and to Margaret's surprise, Penelope was known in many of the fashion houses. This gave them the opportunity to visit the work rooms, and see some of the very expensive gowns being made. It gave Margaret a very warm feeling, reminding her of her Mother, and of how she used to work.

In one of the establishments, the proprietor was quite an elderly, but distinguished lady, Madame Henri. She instantly liked this young and very attractive English girl, and asked if she would model for her. Margaret was thrilled to be asked. Penelope agreed and thought it a tremendous idea, and an insight into couture clothes for Margaret. It was decided Margaret would model two outfits. One, a day suit, and the other, a cocktail dress. The problem arose just before the show was about to start. Madame Henri didn't think that Margaret's name was suitable for a catwalk model. In an instant, she clicked her fingers and renamed her, 'Maggie'. With Madame Henri's French accent it sounded lovely - 'Maggie' it was.

The second week of their holiday was as exciting as the first. They were staying in Milan and Rome. Penelope had as many business contacts based in Milan as in Paris. She didn't like to admit it, but the holiday was much easier to plan without Margery going. On the middle Saturday, they took a train from Paris to Milan.

Christine Friend

Penelope and Maggie spent Sunday and Monday catching up with Penelope's contacts. Tuesday, they were back on the train to Rome. For Maggie, she enjoyed Paris, but Rome came alive for her. There was a lot to see, and she was completely captivated with the Vatican. She had never shown any real interest in religion, but it was the splendour and style of the buildings that really interested her.

All too soon, the holiday was over. All of Penelope's business contacts had been very generous to Maggie, as if she had been a daughter. Maggie had selected some of the outfits for herself, but had put aside almost half for Margery. If they fitted and suited Maggie, then the same would go for Margery. In Rome, extra luggage had to be bought, which was also needed for the presents that Maggie had bought for family and friends.

The flight from Rome would have them back at London airport at 3pm, and then a taxi to take them to St. Albans.

Maggie noticed the drop in temperature as they descended the aeroplane steps. It already had the feel of autumn. A familiar sense of reality was starting to drift back over her, but she was so looking forward to seeing Margery that she couldn't feel disappointed at her holiday being over.

Just after five o'clock, the taxi drove up Penelope's drive. The driver got out, and started to unload the boot, while Penelope sorted out her money to pay the fare. Maggie wasn't sure whether she should pick up her luggage and go next door, but before she could ask

Penelope, Connie had the front door open and was calling both of them in.

"Welcome home, come in Margaret. Let's bring your luggage in. Go into the front room, the kettle is on."

Maggie was a bit surprised now. She had hoped that Margery would have been looking out of their bedroom window waiting for their arrival. She didn't really want to stay and have a cup of tea, but she didn't want to appear ungrateful. She went into the front room, and as she sat down, the door was pushed closed behind her. She could hear Connie speaking to Penelope in a hushed voice. The door opened, and Penelope was standing there holding an envelope. Maggie was now beginning to feel worried, was someone ill? Was it Margery?

"Maggie, while we were away, a lot has happened next door. Mrs Barnes has left this for you. You see, they have gone to Harrogate."

"To Harrogate? What for, a holiday? Where is Margery?"

"Apparently Mrs Barnes has explained in full in this letter, but I understand from Connie that Mr Barnes was transferred there during our first week away. I think it would be best to read the letter."

Maggie opened the envelope and began to read.

## Christine Friend

*Dear Margaret,*
*I am sure this will come as a big surprise to you just as it was to us. Uncle Edward has been transferred to the Harrogate branch of the bank. The post had to be taken up immediately, so we are living in rented accommodation, found for us by the bank.*
*Since we have been here, Margery has been very lucky and has found herself a job in the University of York, working in one of their libraries.*
*I know this will have come as a big shock to you, but I am sure when you get up here we will be able to get you another suitable job, there are a number of big departmental stores around.*
*We hope you had a good holiday, and perhaps you could write to us so that we know when to expect you,*
*Fondest love*
*Aunt Edith*

Maggie handed the letter to Penelope to read. She felt as though someone had punched her hard in the stomach. She wanted to cry, but felt so completely drained she just didn't have the energy. Connie gave Maggie a handkerchief. She had some idea as to what was in the letter, as Edna had filled her in before they left.

Penelope replaced the letter in the envelope and sat next to Maggie.

When Life Changes Direction

"You know you can stay here for as long as you like? Tomorrow we will go over everything and look at all the scenarios, and then go from there."
It was all too much, Penelope being so kind, Aunt Edith, being so beastly and Margery... What was Margery doing, moving away and not demanding to stay? The sobs and tears started, and Maggie's little hunched up body shook. Penelope took her in her arms, devastated to see Maggie so upset and hurt.
That evening passed in a haze for Maggie. She eventually stopped crying, but now her head was throbbing. Her eyes felt very puffy and sore. Connie had realised during the week that Maggie would be staying with them for the immediate future. She had purchased lamb chops for their supper, and at great expense too, as meat was still rationed. Maggie barely touched hers, and Penelope and Connie felt theirs stick in their throats. It was after they had finished supper that Maggie asked to see the letter again. Penelope wasn't so sure it was such a good idea, but while playing with her food, something had crossed Maggie's mind.
She held the letter up.
"Look, Aunt Edith hasn't even left an address. How I am supposed to get in contact, or even find them?"
Connie answered,
"Mrs Barnes left the address separately, and also a front door key. She thought you might need some of your clothes, and things for work."
Maggie looked in disbelief.

"She doesn't have any plans for me to go to Harrogate. She has got what she wanted, and that's *Margery*."
Maggie stomped upstairs to the guest room.
Later on, Penelope took some hot milk up to her. Maggie was already in bed. She was sitting up and looked extremely fragile. Penelope didn't want to upset her. There had been enough tears for one day, but she could understand how sad she must feel.
"Maggie, tomorrow we will talk and you can decide what you want to do. I will do my best to sort this out for you. I know this is going to be hard, but do try to get some sleep. Good night."
"Thank you Penelope - I always knew Aunt Edith disliked me, I just didn't realise how much."
"Come on Maggie, I am sure that isn't true. No more talking. It's been a long day."
Penelope went back downstairs to find Connie, who was in the kitchen washing up the milk saucepan.
"That wasn't how I thought our holiday was going to end. We had such a good time. Everyone was so generous to her. I just hope coming home to this won't taint all of her memories."
Connie looked round.
"You know it might to start, but she is a bright girl. What's this, calling her 'Maggie'?"
"Do you remember me mentioning Madame Henri? Well, we met up with her in Paris, and she thought that 'Maggie' was more friendly, and suited her personality more."
"Well I know one person who won't like it"

"Connie, if you are referring to Mrs Barnes, I happen to think that it won't matter to her *what* Maggie is called."

## *Chapter Eighteen*

Maggie had a restless night, and still felt tired when she woke up but knew she couldn't stay in bed any longer. By 6.30am, she was washed and dressed. Connie announced breakfast at 8am, which all three ate in the dining room. When they had all finished, Connie got up to clear away, but Penelope had other plans.
"I think the sooner we sit down and discuss what is to be done, the better. Let's just clear the table, then the three of us can make plans."
Connie looked surprised to be included, and pointed this out.
"Connie, three heads are better than two, and unless Maggie has any objections..."
"Please stay, Connie. I value your impartiality."
Said Maggie, with a wry smile on her face, the first hint of normality since they had arrived home.

All three sat around the dining table as though it was a business meeting. Penelope took control by asking Maggie if she had any idea what she would like to do. Maggie was quite clear she didn't want to live in Harrogate. She didn't want to give her job up, but for her to do this where could she live?
Penelope was hoping this was going to be the answer, although she feared this would make her seem as controlling as Mrs Barnes.

When Life Changes Direction

"That is easy". Penelope answered.
"You live here with Connie and myself. There are two spare bedrooms you can choose which one you would like. Today we will get your things from next door that you need for work. We have the luggage to sort out. That does include presents and the clothes made for Margery. I would also suggest you write to the Barnes' today, and explain your immediate plans. You can also ask if, and when they may be coming back to sort the house out. That way, we will be able to work out how you are going to give them the presents etc. Maggie, I don't want you to worry, it will all workout."

Sunday was a busy day for everyone. Connie, who never did washing on a Sunday, thought this was an exception. The weather was still warm, but blowy, an excellent day for getting washing dry. It was decided that the big meal of the day would be in the evening. And so, at lunchtime, Penelope went to the kitchen and made sandwiches and a large pot of tea.

Going into next door felt very strange for Maggie. To start with, she had never had her own front door key, so to be letting herself in felt very odd.

She was surprised to see various things missing; clocks, ornaments and all the Barnes personnel mementos. In some ways, it did prepare her for entering the bedroom which she had shared with Margery. She expected to only see her personal things around, and yes, Margery's Knick knacks had all gone, but she still felt shocked. Both single beds had been stripped, leaving them ready for moving.

In all the time the girls had lived with the Barnes', she had only ever been in their bedroom a handful of times, but now she felt the need to see what had been removed. To her dismay, it had been cleared - except for the heavy bedroom furniture. How could all of this have been organised in the few days after she had left for Europe with Penelope? It was then that she remembered Aunt Edith and Uncle Edward kissing her goodbye, something they had never done before. This move had been planned for some time. Well there was absolutely no way was she going to write to Mrs Barnes now, not if it meant appearing wanting. Maggie wouldn't give her that satisfaction.

## *Chapter Nineteen*

Nothing much happened for the next four weeks. Maggie went back to work and, although she now lived with Penelope, she still went to the station at her regular time. This meant travelling there on her own, as Penelope always set out an hour earlier. Coming back home to St. Albans was different, as Penelope tried to ensure that they travelled together.
Maggie had hoped that Margery would have written to her, but realised she was not only lazy, but weak. She did want to write herself, but wasn't sure if Mrs Barnes would pass on the letter. As well as that, she was still hurt - and angry with Margery.

On the Tuesday evening, when they returned home, there was a letter waiting for Maggie. It was a good quality envelope, and inside was matching paper. She opened it to see the name and address of a solicitor in St. Albans High Street. It was formally written, and informed her that any belongings she may still have at 40 Larkswood Avenue would have to be removed by Friday week, as that was the day the new owners were moving in. Anything left would be taken to Harrogate. Maggie was stunned. She handed the letter to Penelope to read.
Penelope's face said it all.
"Maggie, don't worry. Don't come into work tomorrow. Connie will help you. It's best to remove your things

now, as we don't know when the removal men will arrive and start to pack. It doesn't look like the Barnes' will be coming back at all. Have you anything big to be moved?"
"It's really only clothes and books and things. I didn't realise a house could be sold so quickly."
Penelope, who up until now had tried to remain neutral, added,
"It normally takes a lot longer, because there are generally a number of properties involved. It does make me wonder how long this has been going on for? I do think that perhaps you should write, if not to Mrs Barnes, then to Margery. Mr and Mrs Barnes behaviour has been appalling, but if you don't it could cause a rift between you girls."
"OK, I will write. But only because *you* are asking me to."

She sat down that evening and wrote a brief note to her sister;

When Life Changes Direction

*42 Larkswood Avenue
St. Albans*

*7$^{th}$ October 1952*

*Dear Margery
I hope you are all keeping well.
Some business contacts of Penelope's very generously made you and I some winter dresses. As they are suitable to be worn soon, how shall I get them and my holiday presents to you?
Love from*

*Maggiexx*

Maggie showed Penelope her letter. Penelope couldn't help but smile.
"I see you decided to make it quite brief".
"I am still angry with her. I have tried not to be, but why hasn't she written to me? Either before they moved, or after."
Penelope did agree but didn't want to start a big discussion again. It wouldn't help.

Five days later Maggie received a reply.

Christine Friend

*10th October 1952*

*Dear Margaret,*
*We are all well here, hope you are too. As the removal men will be packing up 40 Larkswood Avenue next week, could you put anything you have for me in a box and hand it to them?*
*I was hoping you would join us up here. It is very nice and I am enjoying my new job.*
*We are moving into our new house on Wednesday 22nd October. Perhaps it would be better if you addressed any further letters there.*

*The Nest*
*16 Laurel Crescent*
*Harrogate*
*Yorkshire*

*Love from*
*Margery xx*

Maggie tried to read her letter without getting upset, but she found it so hard. No one had given her any thought at all. The fact that Mrs Barnes had not written again proved how little she was included. Margery knew how much she enjoyed her job with Penelope, and to find another with the same prospects would be impossible. Mrs Barnes clearly had no idea what her job entailed if she thought that working in a departmental store was an equivalent. What was also bothering Maggie, was the worry of how much longer Penelope would let her stay in her house.

After supper that evening, she passed her letter to Penelope to read. After reading it, she placed it back in the envelope and handed it back.

"Maggie, I think it is time for you to plan your future. Mr and Mrs Barnes are not being very helpful, so you are in a position to choose your own destiny. I suppose we must look at how you see your career. I am being a bit selfish because I don't want you to leave, but you are giving up a lot by staying here; living with your family, namely your sister. If you were to stay, then I am hoping that this will become your home. It's a huge decision and not something to take lightly. If you would like to go and stay in Harrogate and look for another job then it wouldn't be a problem - you would always be welcome back if it didn't work out."

Maggie looked at Penelope, and realised for the first time that she was the only person who really cared about her. Margery and Mr and Mrs Barnes had all put themselves first. If she did go to Harrogate and it didn't work out then it would seem as though she was making Penelope her second choice. Since Margery and the Barnes had moved, they hadn't even asked if she was well, or when she was going to Harrogate. Or even how her holiday had been? Maggie didn't think there was a choice to be made.

"Penelope, if you will have me, then I really would like to stay here and carry on working with you. I will go to Harrogate and perhaps stay for Christmas, but I need to think about my future. I still can't get out of my mind the fact that Mrs Barnes could have planned this whole thing just so that she could have the one she really wanted."

Penelope held her hands out to Maggie.

"Now your future is all sorted, let's go and find Connie. I know she will be just as delighted as I am."

They went to the kitchen where Connie was making a pot of tea.

"Connie, I have the best news, Maggie is staying!"

Connie put down the teapot and gave Maggie a hug, and said,

"I'm sure we will all be very happy living here."

Penelope went to the dresser drawer, and took out a little package which she handed to Maggie. "This is from Connie and myself."

When Maggie opened it, she was holding her first front door key.

Penelope continued,

"This is your home now, so you must come and go as you like. The only suggestion that I would like to make, is that maybe you should see more young people? Why don't you look up your old school friends? They all still live locally, and if at any time you go out and it gets late, then you can ask your friends to stay over. Do you remember when I told you that I had lost my parents? Well, I went and lived with my Grandmother during the holidays as I was at boarding school, and she encouraged me to make good friends. Whom, I might add, I am still friends with today…and that isn't just because I sell them nice clothes."

When Life Changes Direction

Maggie laughed. She already knew a lot of Penelope's old school friends from the shops.

The house next door was emptied, and a new family, with three young children moved in.

Maggie's bedroom was redecorated and furnished, and at Christmas, Maggie went to Harrogate. Margery was pleased to see her, but as the days went by, Margery drifted back into her books. Mr and Mrs Barnes were polite, but didn't put much effort into her stay. She was sad to say goodbye to Margery, but promised to go again when the weather improved. She also asked Margery if she would write more often, as she loved receiving her letters. She stayed for six days and returned on the 30$^{th}$ December. What Maggie found sadder, was that once she was back on the train heading for London, her spirits rose. In some ways she was regretting not having stayed in St.Albans for Christmas. She was sure she would have had much more fun.
On her arrival at 42 Larkswood Avenue, she opened the front door to see a hive of industry. Penelope and Connie had spent the day moving furniture around for a party they had planned for New Year's Eve. Maggie didn't even know that New Year's Eve was celebrated, and couldn't wait to get involved.

## *Chapter Twenty*

For Maggie, the next few years followed a pattern. One week in June Maggie would go on her annual visit to Harrogate. She didn't particularly enjoy the venture. She found it very stuffy, and it reminded her of being back in school. It wasn't that Penelope allowed her total freedom at home, but she did treat her as an adult and, as such, gave her privacy and independence. When she arrived in Harrogate at Aunt Edith's and Uncle Edward's, she was constantly asking permission. Would it be okay to have a bath? Would it be alright to make a cup of tea? Would it be an inconvenience for her and Margery to go to a tearoom for tea? Maggie found she was met with the most resistance when asking about going to the cinema, with only her twin sister. Aunt Edith was most put out, as she explained that Margery always went to the pictures with them. As it was coming to the end of her stay, she couldn't help herself saying "It will be a nice change for Margery to go with someone else then."

As well as this break, Maggie also spent two weeks in Europe with Penelope each year. They had enjoyed their holiday so much the first time, that this is what they did in subsequent years. The holidays would always incorporate some shopping, sightseeing and an opportunity for Penelope to catch up with business acquaintances. While they were away, Connie would take herself off to Eastbourne for two weeks. She would always stay in the same guest house, and visit the same tea shops. By the time her holiday was finished, she would have revamped her wardrobe with at least three cardigans that she would have knitted while away.

After Penelope's initial encouragement, Maggie now had a number of very close girlfriends. During the week, Maggie often worked late - either helping to change the window displays, or telephoning clients who were never available during the day. She found it hard to join anything on a regular basis, but on a Sunday she belonged to a cycle club. This, she thoroughly enjoyed - cycling for miles, and then stopping for refreshments. The cycle club was mixed, and Maggie was always in demand when a dance was being organised. But she felt that to commit and have a serious boyfriend, would somehow be letting Penelope down. Penelope had put a lot of trust in her. There was also this nagging feeling that her Mother, Agnes, had never really fulfilled her own potential, and Maggie still felt after all the years since her death that she wanted to do well, and make Agnes proud.

## *Chapter Twenty One*

Maggie and Margery celebrated their 21$^{st}$ birthday on Tuesday 18$^{th}$ January 1955. Not the best day of the week for a party, but it worked well as Maggie had travelled to Harrogate so that she should share it with her twin sister. Then she could be back on the Friday to celebrate it at the weekend with Penelope and Connie. They had promised her a surprise, and Maggie was hoping it was going to be one of Penelope's legendary parties.

This was going to be Maggie's annual trip to Harrogate. After she went the first time at Christmas, she decided that it would suit her better in future to go in the summer. That way, Margery and herself weren't confined to be indoors with Mr and Mrs Barnes. However, she was prepared to break this rule for their special birthday. Maggie may have put herself out more if Margery had been willing to come and visit herself sometimes, but she always made the excuse that she didn't feel confident enough to travel on her own.

As Maggie had expected, she felt she was in the way, and as always, Mrs Barnes never made her feel very welcome. When it came to opening their birthday presents, there were two small boxes - one for each of them, from Mr and Mrs Barnes. The girls opened them excitedly; inside Maggie's was a pretty brooch in a yellow gold metal, with paste stones. She thanked Mr and Mrs Barnes. Then Margery opened hers. It was clear that Margery's was not a fake. It was a flower design again, but it was made of gold, and was set with garnets, the girls birthday stone. Margery was thrilled, and Maggie was sure she had no idea of the discrepancy in the presents.

Edna loved the girls equally, and although Maggie no longer lived with them, she treated them the same. She had bought them both an expensive fountain pen. On the gold clip, she had their names engraved. When Mrs Barnes looked, she gave a grunt on seeing the inscription 'Maggie' had been engraved, in favour of 'Margaret'.

The previous day, two rather large boxes had been delivered. One addressed to each of the girls. This time they opened them simultaneously. Inside the boxes were cream, leather weekend cases. The cases were lined with a very pale, shell pink satin. They oozed luxury and expense. With them, was a card - they could only have been from one person, Penelope. Maggie looked at Mrs Barnes.

"Aunt Edith, aren't they exquisite! And how much fun for Margery and I to have been given exactly the same."

The day itself was very cold, but the highlight was to have a birthday lunch at the nearby hotel. The hotel restaurant was very nice, but Maggie found there was no sparkle. In between courses Mrs Barnes made a remark that left Maggie feeling left out.

"Margery, isn't it all rather special here. Just the place for a wedding breakfast."

Maggie looked up at Mrs Barnes, and then at Margery, who was looking decidedly uncomfortable.

She wasn't going to get upset today, two can play at that game.

"Oh Margery, that's great. You are a quiet one, come on, tell me all about him."

Margery, looking extremely embarrassed, felt she had no option but to fill Maggie in.

"Nothing is decided at the moment. I met Donald last summer at the University library. He is a translator and works in the civil service. At the moment he is working in Nuremberg. He is flying back on Friday, and then coming to Harrogate on Saturday to take me out to lunch. Aunt Edith thinks it is to propose…"

Luckily, at that moment, Margery caught sight of the head waiter walking towards their table carrying a birthday cake.

For now the conversation was over.

It wasn't until the Thursday afternoon, Maggie's last day before she travelled home when, she took Margery to Betty's tea shop for afternoon tea. This was Maggie's treat, and she was going to have Margery all to herself.

"Margery, now we are on our own, tell me all about Donald."

When Life Changes Direction

Rather sheepishly, Margery told her of how she met him at the library. That he was very clever, extremely good looking -although he wasn't aware of it himself - and that he made her feel special, and not self-conscious - unlike other young men that she had met had done. As always, Maggie was very pleased for her sister and wished for her everything that she wished for herself - adding that she had yet to be lucky enough meet the man of her dreams.

Again as Maggie sat in the carriage on the train home she was deflated by her trip. It seemed every visit she made to Harrogate, Margery became more complacent. She hoped for her sister's sake that Donald would propose. Perhaps if she were to get married, and get away from Aunt Edith's clutches, she would have a happier life. Maggie was convinced that Margery wasn't happy now.

As Maggie had hoped, a party had been planned on the Saturday.
It was just before the guests started to arrive that Penelope gave her another present. She handed her a gift box. Maggie opened it, inside there was a beautiful gold watch. On closer inspection, Maggie could see that it was a ladies Rolex, with an ivory white dial and crocodile strap. She was speechless. She had seen a few of the clientele wearing this brand, and she knew that it was very expensive.
Penelope could see the shock on her face.

"Maggie, I have come to look on you as the daughter I have never had. When I was young, I was terrified in being tied down, married. I have always enjoyed my freedom, which when you're young is good, but when you came to live here I realised what I had missed out on because of those choices. In my time I have had many serious boyfriends, and hope that I will continue to until my dotage, but you will always come first. Now let's try it on for size before your guests arrive."
Maggie held out her wrist and Penelope put the watch on. It fitted perfectly. Maggie put her arms around this glamorous lady, who had given her the love that previously only her Mother and Grandmother had shown her.

## *Chapter Twenty Two*

Margery

As always when Maggie is visiting, Aunt Edith always manages to say the wrong thing. When I looked across and saw the hurt in Maggie's eyes, for one minute I did think Aunt Edith had deliberately set out to upset her. It wasn't her place to say that I might be getting engaged soon.

When I look back, it all happened so fast. One minute we were all living in St. Albans and the next, Aunt Edith, Uncle Edward and I had moved to Harrogate. It is just as nice here, and if we hadn't moved I wouldn't have met Donald, but I still miss Maggie terribly. I had been looking forward to telling Maggie all about Donald myself.
When Maggie arrived on Monday, the day before our twenty first birthday, she asked Aunt Edith what had been arranged. Once Aunt Edith had told us of her plans, Maggie announced that her birthday treat to me was tea at Betty's on Thursday afternoon, the day before she returned to St. Albans. Aunt Edith took exception to the fact that Maggie would want to see me on my own. Instantly, there seemed to be an atmosphere, and I feel I am walking on eggshells. I wonder if getting older makes women possessive, because that is how it feels. I realise that Maggie and I

were very lucky to have been billeted with Aunt and Uncle. What would have happened to us after Mummy had been killed?

Now Aunt Edith has caused another problem.
Donald did propose to me the weekend after my twenty first birthday. It was so exciting and romantic. We went out to lunch in a restaurant in Knaresborough. Just before we ordered dessert, Donald got down on one knee and asked me to marry him - I was so excited I accepted immediately! He had even come prepared with an engagement ring. It is so pretty. Three diamonds, set in white gold on a yellow gold band. It is a little loose, so it is back at the jewellers being resized.

Once we left the restaurant we jumped straight back on the train to Harrogate and went home to show Aunt Edith and Uncle Edward my ring, but they already knew he was going to propose. Donald had written to Uncle Edward a few weeks before to ask his permission. When we got back, there was tea already set, and Mr and Mrs Green were there, Donald's parents.

It has already been decided that the wedding should take place in September. Mrs Green asked if I was going to have any bridesmaids and before I could answer, Aunt Edith, in a very quiet voice suggested that it would probably be best not to, as it wouldn't be possible to ask my sister. With this, Mrs Green and Aunt Edith exchanged a knowing look, and the subject was dropped. How can I write to Maggie now and tell her my news? I am just hoping that she will write and ask me in a way that will embarrass Aunt Edith. Then maybe she will back down, and Maggie - and perhaps even Penelope - will be there on my big day.

## *Chapter Twenty Three*

Maggie had decided that on this occasion she was going to wait for Margery to write and announce her special news. Not out of jealousy, Maggie just felt it was time her sister made more effort in their relationship. The months went by, and Maggie still hadn't had any news from her sister, so she thought that perhaps Aunt Edith had got it wrong. But now she didn't think it appropriate for her to write. She would give her until July, then she would contact her, and make a summer visit in August or September.

As it happened, none of Maggie's plans came to fruition. On a Monday morning in May while getting ready for work, she became doubled up in pain. Penelope had already left so as to catch the earlier train. Connie immediately rang the Doctor. By time he arrived in the late morning, Maggie was in a more comfortable state, so he asked Connie to ring him immediately if it occurred again and he would come straight out. By the afternoon, Maggie was doubled up again. Connie did as the Doctor asked, and he arrived this time in ten minutes. Five minutes later, he was ringing for an ambulance. He suspected peritonitis. While this was going on, Connie packed a bag with toiletries and nightie. No sooner had she finished, the ambulance was there and she had no time to phone Penelope. She travelled with Maggie in the ambulance. On their arrival at St Albans General Hospital, Maggie was examined, given morphine and whisked off to theatre.

Connie made her way to the public telephone.

"Penelope, it is Connie, I am at St. Albans General. It's Maggie - they think she has peritonitis and they have taken her straight into theatre."

Before Connie could finish, Penelope spoke over her.

"I am leaving now. I don't know what train I will be on, but wait for me. Don't leave her."

The telephone went dead, and Connie made her way back to the seating area to wait for the two most important people in her life; one to arrive by train, and one to return from the theatre in a better state than she went in.

Connie couldn't remember how long she sat there before the Surgeon came and spoke,

"Miss Smith, I am relieved to say she has survived the surgery, but I am afraid the infection had already spread, and infected part of her reproductive system. We have had to perform a hysterectomy, as well as an appendectomy. She is very weak, and even at this stage, I don't know if she is clear from infection."

The surgeon, seeing the tears falling from her eyes, called a nurse over and asked her to take Connie to the ward that Maggie had been put on.

Connie sat by her bedside in the ward side room from 9 in the morning, until 8 at night, while Maggie drifted in out of sleep. Sometimes she opened her eyes and asked for Penelope, but within seconds they would be closed again. By the fourth day, Maggie opened her eyes as though waking from a deep sleep. She saw

Connie sitting by the bed. In a very quiet voice, she spoke,
"Connie, it's you who has been sitting there - I couldn't make out who it was."
She looked across to the door.
"Is Penelope at work?"
Connie gripped the handles of her handbag, which was resting on her lap.
"Maggie, something terrible has happened."
Maggie recognised those words from when she was a little girl. The tears started to fall from Maggie's eyes.
"Where is she Connie? She is alright?!"
"Maggie, Penelope was involved in an accident on the way to the hospital on Monday, I am so sorry - she was killed."
Maggie's scream was heart wrenching. Within seconds, the Sister of the ward and a junior nurse ran into the room. Connie was trying to stop Maggie from sitting up. The Sister immediately took control, and spoke in an authoritative voice, telling Maggie to lie down. Whether she was doing as she was told, or just exhausted from the distress and struggle, Connie didn't know. The Sister turned to Connie.
"I am assuming you have told her. Thank you, it was a big ask of you that the Doctors made."
A while later, the sister returned, "Now Maggie, I can give you something to make you feel a bit calmer. It won't make you sleep. You have had to have a lot of surgery and once you have managed to have something to eat, we would like to get you up and out

of bed. Today is Friday, and you do need to start moving around."

Maggie- listening to the Sister - seemed to calm down, and then answered,

"I don't want any drugs, I just want Penelope, and to go home, and that's never going to happen again."

This time, the crying was quieter. The Sister and nurse gently sat her up, and plumped up her pillows for her to rest back on.

"Are you in any pain now, because if you are you must tell us so we can make you as comfortable as possible?"

"Thank you Sister, my stomach feels really sore and to the right of it as well. What have I had done?"

"Let's not dwell on that now. You have had a terrible shock. I will get you something for the pain, and then perhaps at lunchtime you might be able to manage some soup. Miss Smith can stay with you."

Turning to Connie, she said,

"Miss Smith, if Maggie needs anything please come and let me know. Perhaps when it is lunchtime you might like a break. One of my nurses will be at hand to offer any assistance."

It was another week before Maggie's surgeon explained to her fully the surgery that she had undergone. Connie and the Sister were both very supportive to her, but it was heart breaking to see. Just as she was starting to come to terms with the news about Penelope, she was being told that she had to have a hysterectomy, and could never experience the joy of carrying a child. Her surgeon, Mr Hall, made it clear that they had no options - her condition had been life threatening.

Maggie's future suddenly felt so bleak. No children. Probably no husband either.

At week three, Maggie was spending sometime out of bed, in the armchair. Connie was still spending most of the day with her. She would tentatively mention Penelope's funeral, but Maggie would turn away, as if doing so meant it wasn't going to happen.

Penelope's Solicitor was in constant contact with Connie as - according to Penelope's will - it was down to him to make all the arrangements for her funeral. When the subject was mentioned at the beginning to Maggie, she made it clear that she couldn't, and wouldn't attend.

Connie found the ward Sister very approachable, and asked her advice. Had she ever come across a similar situation? Sister's advice was just to "give her time." "If she doesn't go, she will undoubtedly regret it in the future." Sister also informed them both that at the end of the fourth week, her Surgeon was happy for her to be discharged. With this news, Connie tried again, and pointed out that Maggie was Penelope's Chief mourner and it may appear disrespectful if she wasn't there. What Connie had never given any thought to, was why she didn't want to be there. Maggie revealed that she was terrified that someone might actually accuse her of Penelope's death.

"But Maggie, why would you think that?"

"If I hadn't been ill, she wouldn't have been on her way to the Hospital."
"You must never blame yourself. You made Penelope very happy, from that first moment, during the war, that you spoke to her over the garden fence. When you moved in with us, she felt you were the daughter she had never had. Look, dry your eyes. I will leave earlier today and go and see the Solicitor, or leave a message with his secretary. I think it would be best if he could start to make the arrangements for the end of the week, when you are discharged."
The arrangements were made for the Friday, and the wake would be held at Larkswood Avenue.


Her first week home was extremely busy. Maureen, whom had taken over as temporary Manageress at both of Penelope's establishments had come to visit. She asked Maggie what she would be wearing as Chief mourner, and representing Penelope. There would certainly be a lot of people in the trade attending, and many clients. Maggie shrugged. She was feeling far too sad and delicate to feel that clothes were important. Maureen had come prepared. She had bought with her a black silk dress. It had a round neck, fitted under the bust line to the waist, and then a full skirt. But, thinking of Maggie's surgery, the waist had been loosened. To go with it, was a black swagger coat, also in silk. Maureen didn't think she would want to wear a hat, so she had made a bandeau that would be worn from just behind her fringe to the crown. Maggie was amazed. The clothes looked stunning, and yet still felt comfortable despite all her surgery. She thanked Maureen profusely for thinking of her.

The day itself was a glorious summer's day. Maggie was in the first car with Connie and Penelope's only true relation, her late brother's wife. Patricia was well known to Maggie, as she often frequented her sister-in-law's shops. The second car had six of Penelope's closest friends. Two of which were former boyfriends. The service and graveside proved to be almost too much for Maggie. When they returned to Larkswood Avenue, she was mentally and physically exhausted, but pushed herself to thank everybody who attended. The mourners, with the exception of Connie, Patricia and the Solicitor, gradually filtered away. By now it was almost 3pm, and Maggie was hoping for a lay down, but she could see the Solicitor was hovering.
"Miss Bailey, is there somewhere we could sit and talk? I do have something rather important to discuss with you."
This was all she needed. Was she to be made homeless? And possibly, jobless?
They were standing in the front room, so she took him to the dining room where they sat at the table.
Mr Williams spoke.
"It is regarding Miss Waltham's will."
Mr Williams continued and, the more he spoke, the more shock Maggie felt.

"Miss Bailey, you do understand everything I have said? I can see it has been a lot for you take in."
"Yes it certainly has. Are you saying that - other than personal bequests, and money to Connie - she's left her business, property, investments, Jewellery, and personnel affects, all to me? I am stunned. I don't know what to say."
"Miss Bailey, Miss Waltham has made you a wealthy lady. If you would like me to arrange a sum of money for the immediate future, that would be very easy to arrange. I will leave you now. It has been a long day for you. When you are ready, make an appointment and I will go through everything with you."

As soon as Mr Williams left, Maggie made her way upstairs to her bedroom. All she wanted to do was cry. To think that Penelope had left her so much somehow didn't seem right, but she was so sad, and so tired. She took off her shoes, laid on the bed and instantly fell asleep.
She awoke to hear a tapping on her door. She called out, "come in" and Patricia entered.
"Maggie, how are you? Would you like some supper? Connie has just put a Cottage pie into the oven. It smells delicious."
"I will try. She goes to so much effort to make me eat. Before we go down Patricia, can I ask you something?"
"Of course dear, what is it?"
"Well, Penelope has left me practically all her estate. I am so shocked. Can you think of anyone she may have missed out?"

Patricia laughed.
"Penelope confided in me before she made her will. She had a feeling you would feel uncomfortable with her gesture. My advice is to spend it wisely. She had a lot faith and trust in you. Maggie, you are aware how much she loved you? You really did become the daughter she never had."

## *Chapter Twenty Four*

The next seven months were an uphill struggle for Maggie. Her grief was so over whelming at times that she found it hard to focus on anything. Her recovery from all her surgery was very slow. Had it not been for Connie, who was patient, and looked after and cared for her, Maggie would have felt totally alone. Everyone in her life whom she had loved had left her; her Mother, her Grandmother, and now Penelope Waltham, her surrogate Mother. Then there was Margery, her identical twin whom she had not heard from since their $21^{st}$ birthdays. She felt so betrayed by her. When people realised she was a twin, they always wrongly assumed that they were close. If you were close, should there not be some sort of telepathy between you? Surely Margery knew her sister needed her!

Maureen, who was managing both shops, visited Maggie twice a month. On those visits she bought news of all the staff. Most had been to visit Maggie themselves. More importantly, Maureen used these visits to gently ease Maggie back into the running of the business. A lot of the staff were worried for their jobs, and Maureen knew it was down to her, the Solicitor Mr Williams and the business accountant to make Maggie feel capable and confident. Fortunately, Maggie was a fast learner, and although not yet well enough to go to work, she enjoyed the meetings - if

only because it made her feel useful - and it would temporarily take her out of her tunnel of grief.
In the November, Maggie had a hospital appointment with her Surgeon, Mr Hall. She had a thorough examination, and he was pleased to see her looking so well.
Frequently, many of the nursing staff in recent months had asked if he knew how she was. Her devastating story had circulated the hospital. At 21, having to have a hysterectomy was bad enough. But to tragically lose her guardian on the same day didn't bear thinking about.
He was a kind man, and in some way he felt responsible for her future childless state. He had reconciled that it had been the only way to save her life, but even to him it seemed to be so final.
He felt he should allay any fears that she might have about her future.
"Maggie, you have recovered extremely well. This may not be of any consolation now, but the surgery you have had should not stop you from ever getting married and having a full married life. The only effect it will have is that you won't be able to fall pregnant. Of course, you are still very young, and may have not ever thought about marriage and babies. My daughter has been in a similar position, so I can talk from a certain amount of experience. She and her husband have decided to adopt", he paused, "I do hope I haven't spoken out of turn?"
"Mr Hall, I know you are being kind but this year my whole life has been turned upside down."

She couldn't look at him because she knew she was going to get emotional.

"At the moment, I am trying to concentrate on getting back to work. Since Penelope died, I have been given an immense amount of responsibility. I guess it wasn't easy for you, but thank you. I know you saved my life."

She got up to leave before the tears started, holding out her hand to shake his, then swiftly turning around and hurriedly walking out.

The nurse who was assisting him in clinic was welling up, and to her surprise heard Mr Hall utter to himself, "A most remarkable young woman."

## *Chapter Twenty Five*

Maggie's business in the following years went from strength to strength. Knowing Penelope's ambition was to expand, Maggie decided that she would keep to the two stores. She didn't want to over stretch herself, she was concerned that they would lose their reputation for personal service with any form of expansion.
She had a really good eye for knowing when fashions were going to last and when they wouldn't take off, and this made her invaluable to her clients.

It was now April, 1960. She now only saw the most prestigious clients, and on this particular Monday morning she was in the South Kensington shop helping a testing client to choose numerous items of clothing for a cruise, when she was interrupted by Maureen, her deputy manageress,
"I am very sorry to interrupt Maggie, but there is rather an important phone call for you. It has come through for you on your office phone."
Maureen could see that Maggie was not amused. She was dealing with a difficult customer who always spent a lot of money with them.
Maggie spoke,
"Maureen, did the caller give their name?"
"Yes she did, Mrs Margery Green."
Maggie raised her eyebrow.

"I am sorry Maureen, the name doesn't really mean anything to me. Could you take her number and I will call her back."
Maureen nodded and disappeared. Within seconds she was back, but this time she whispered into Maggie's ear.
"It is your sister, and she says it's urgent."
Maggie instantly put the tape measure down, apologised to the customer and asked Maureen to take over, assuring her that she wouldn't be long.

*Part Two*

## *Chapter Twenty Six*

2<sup>nd</sup> February 2010

Lucy was not only feeling extremely bored, but emotionally drained. The skiing holiday arranged by her friends to help her get over the two year romance that she'd had with Jake, ended up being a disaster.
Jenny - whom Lucy had known since they were eleven, and was due to accompany her on the trip - had managed to oversleep. Consequently, she missed her flight from Gatwick. Fortunately, they had chosen the popular resort of St. Anton in Austria, and she was able to fly out the following day due to a cancellation. However, she ended up spending most of what was left of her holiday keeping Lucy company in hospital.
Lucy, having been on many skiing holidays with her parents, was by no means a novice skier. In fact, quite the opposite. But while waiting with Gemma and Laura at the nursery slope, a rogue skier ploughed into the back of her, and completely wiped her out. The only thing she remembered was the excruciating pain that was shooting through her right ankle. Within minutes, she was being put into an ambulance on a stretcher, which then sped off to the fracture clinic in the resort. On arrival she was taken straight to x- ray, where it was confirmed she had an ankle fracture. As her condition wasn't life threatening, insurance documents were checked before she was taken into theatre to operate.

The medical team's knowledge of fractures was second to none. In this particular clinic, it was what they most commonly dealt with. The main problem for Lucy was that the injury happened from behind, so she had been taken completely unaware, and therefore she had landed very badly. This was going to be a long recovery period. After her fifth day in hospital, she was flown home. She continued her treatment in her local General hospital in St Albans, Hertfordshire. After a few days, her Consultant thought that provided that she did exactly as she was told, then the best place for her to recover was at home. Lucy could not agree quickly enough. She promised that it would be bed rest all the way when needed, and regular physio. This way all her friends could keep her company, and when they were at work, her mother and her grandparents could take a turn.

For the first couple of days everything went well, and then early on the Saturday morning, the doorbell rang. Ginette, Lucy's Mum, answered the door, and was surprised to see Jake standing there, with a large bunch of flowers, and what looked like a box of chocolates. Ginette asked him in, and after exchanging pleasantries, suggested that he might like to give the flowers and chocolates to Lucy himself.

"That would be great, where is she?"

"She is upstairs, Jake. We did offer to make a bed for her down here, but Lucy decided that if she was in her own room then she wouldn't have to keep bothering me to go and fetch things."

"Is it alright, then, just to go up? The last time we spoke she was very angry with me - she might not want to see me?"
"Of course she would like to see you. Up you go and I will bring up some coffee for you both."
Jake went up the stairs and reluctantly knocked on Lucy's bedroom door.
"Come in, I'm decent."
Jake opened the door and walked in.
Lucy didn't know whether to be pleased, or angry, that he should come to visit. Even though it was four months since they had split, upon seeing his face, she quickly realised that she still wasn't over him. If there was any embarrassment it was quickly relieved by her mother, who came bustling in with a tray laden with a coffee pot, mugs, milk, sugar and a plate of biscuits.
"Thank you, Mum"
Ginette took this as an indication to leave - which she did.
Ten minutes later, Ginette and Roger heard the front door close. They looked at each other in surprise. Surely that wasn't Jake leaving? Roger, Lucy's father, got up.
"I think I will just go and ask Lucy if she has finished with the coffee, something doesn't seem right..."
Ten minutes later, Roger was back in the kitchen calling his wife
"Ginny!"
"Just coming"
She stepped back into the kitchen from the utility room,

"Where is the tray?" she asked.
Roger was feeling quite upset.
"Forget the tray, you need to go up to Lucy. That idiot of an ex-boyfriend bought the flowers and chocolates as a farewell gesture. He is taking a years sabbatical, and going travelling. Exactly what Lucy wanted to do with him 12 months ago. And to make matters worse, he is going with the new 'love of his life', who he has only known for three months! She is distraught. Sorry, but better if you go to her."
Roger and Ginette were the perfect couple, in that they complimented each other's strong points. Roger was the logical thinker, and in testing times could always see the positive side. Ginette realised that he must be out of his depth if he was hoping that she could do better in consoling their daughter, as logic was usually not her strong point.
She hurried upstairs, and found Lucy weeping on her bed. She sat down, and cradled her 26 year old daughter in her arms.



Lucy was emotional, and feeling very low. It didn't take very much for her to get upset. Her parents enlisted the help of her friends, and Ginette's parents, to lift her mood, but no one seemed to be able to help. This carried on for the next four days. Ginette and Roger felt they were walking on egg shells in their own home. Then, at ten o'clock one evening, the telephone rang. Roger went to answer it, and saw that the call was

coming from Lucy, upstairs. With a groan, he picked up the phone expecting to hear more tears. To his surprise, Lucy was almost incoherent due to the speed in which she was talking,
"Dad, can you believe it? I know exactly what I am going to do with all this spare time I have. Wait for it, I am going to research our Family tree. You and Mum can help by telling me everything you know about your families. I have just been watching the most brilliant programme. I am going to go on their website now and see how you get started properly. Isn't it great? I can't wait to get started! Goodnight, going to bed now, early starts for me now."
Roger said goodnight to his daughter, and replaced the receiver. Ginette spoke.
"What was Lucy talking about? I couldn't understand a word shall I go up to her?"
"No, I think we can safely say she is over Jake. A thing of the past".
Ginette breathed a sigh of relief.
"I know it sounds uncharitable, but I am *so* pleased."

By 6.30am the following morning, the Wilkinson house was awake. Lucy could hear her parents talking, and so called out to her Mother, as she desperately wanted to get washed and dressed. She had found it hard to sleep the previous evening, so had stayed up past midnight reading 'the beginners guide to Family History', on the internet. She was very methodical, and made notes as she went along. Since working as a P.A.

to a busy firm of solicitors, she knew that organisation was imperative.

Her Mother knocked on her bedroom door, and Lucy called her in. Once all of Lucy's clean clothes were taken out of the various drawers and cupboards, Ginette helped her daughter to the en- suite, and then left Lucy to it.

Ginette was passing her own bedroom when Roger came out, looking around as though he was in some kind of bad spy film. Ginette laughed,

"What's the matter, you do look funny."

Roger straightened his tie.

"I was trying to be sensitive and considerate. How is Lucy this morning? Is she still upbeat or..."

"Or what?" Ginette replied.

"She is fine. In fact she wants to come down to breakfast, so if I were you I would hang around, I don't think it will be long before she calls for help again."

Roger decided to get his tennis kit together while he was waiting for his daughter.

Fifteen minutes later, the Wilkinson family were all down in the kitchen. Ginette was just finishing preparing breakfast, while Lucy was making herself comfortable at the breakfast table.

Once all three of them were sitting down Lucy, filled them in on her new project.

"There was one thing the programme mentioned that should be considered before starting your family history. That is, the chance of finding something out that you might not like."

"Like what?" Roger asked," Did they give you any examples?"

"Oh yes, the main ones being; criminal activity, illegitimacy, bigamy and the workhouse. Apparently, there is a high chance that you will find some of these in all families, and if you don't, then you have probably gone wrong somewhere. So, what I need to ask you both is, do you mind if I try and trace your families? I quite understand if you would rather I didn't."

Roger looked across to Ginette to see if he could gauge her reply, but she was busy stirring her cup of tea. He wasn't so sure that his parents would have liked the idea of Lucy trawling through their family's history, but sadly, neither of them were still alive. And as he was an only child, it wouldn't really affect anyone else.

"I think it's a great idea, I haven't any issues. In fact, I have all Nan and Grandad's paperwork, certificates, and photos. We could go through them if you think it will help?"

"That sounds great Dad, thank you".

She turned to her mother.

"How about you, Mum, are you OK for me to do a bit of sleuthing?"

"Yes, I can't see why not. After all, it's history, it isn't as though you can change it. Why not give Granny and Gramps a call, I'm sure they could probably fill in a few gaps for you. I don't know, but they may even have some photos."

"That would be great, Mum, if they did. Thank you, I can see this is going to be so much fun!"

After breakfast, Roger left for the office. He was an engineer, but was now office based. Driving to work, he reflected on the change of mood in his daughter, and was greatly relieved.
Lucy waited until 9.30am before she phoned her Grandparents. She dialled the number, and quickly, the receiver was picked up.
"Hello"
"Hello Gramps, are you waiting for a call? The phone hardly rang"
"Hello Lucy, you sound bright eyed and bushy tailed this morning! I was walking past the hall table as it rang. Did you want to speak to Granny, or am I the lucky one?"
Lucy's Gran had also heard the phone ring, and was now standing next to her husband. They had both been concerned over Lucy's melancholy state, and as Lucy was still speaking, her Grandfather winked at his wife and mouthed to her,
"She sounds better now".
"Gramps, I can speak to either of you. I have decided what I am going to do with all the spare time I have at the moment."
"This does sound intriguing", he replied.
Lucy's Grandmother left her husband to the call, and went back into the kitchen.
"Actually, that is a very good word to use because, I have decided to research my, or – *our* - family history. Dad is going to dig out all of the paperwork he has that belonged to Nan and Grandad, so I am going to start with them. I don't really know how long it all takes, but

then I thought I could do yours and Granny's family. Would that be alright?"
Donald had started to feel a little unsteady, and found himself with his free hand holding on to the table.
"Yes of course, Lucy. We will give you all the help we can."
"Thanks, Gramps! I best go, got lots of reading to do first, bye."
Donald replaced the receiver, and slowly made his way into the kitchen. His wife had started to clear away the breakfast things, and looked up from the breakfast bar.
"Donald, you look as though you have just seen a ghost, what's happened?"
"It's Lucy, she has decided to trace our Family History."

## *Chapter Twenty Seven*

The excitement of Lucy starting her own family tree wasn't shared by her Mother, but because Lucy's state of mind was much improved due to this new venture, she feigned enthusiasm. That night, when Roger got home, Lucy was already waiting in the lounge for him. She called out to him as he entered the front door.
"Dad! I am in here. I have spent most of the day looking on various family history websites for the best place to start. I have already drawn a tree."
By now, Roger was in the lounge looking at all the paperwork Lucy had spread over the large coffee table.
"So Dad, I have already included both lots of Grandparents on Mum's side, and that is as far as I can go because now I am stuck. What I really need, is your parent's details, Grandad's full name, and Nan's full name and maiden name."
Roger was beginning to feel a bit harassed, he had after all just got home, and today had been quite a difficult day at work. But at least Lucy was bright and bubbly, like her old self.
"Lucy, do you know how long before dinner is ready? I was planning to get all Nan and Grandad's paperwork out after dinner."
"Dinner is ready now. Mum said we can eat as soon as you get home, and that will give you and I all evening to go through certificates and paperwork."
"Oh, did she."

Roger raised his eyebrows, and helped his daughter into the kitchen diner for dinner.

Once dinner was over, the family of three stacked the dishwasher, and Lucy hobbled back into the lounge. Ginette made coffee to bring through to them, and Roger made his way upstairs to bring the fairly large suitcase down, with the papers and photos.

The evening passed very quickly. Ginette, who had never shown any interest, was totally captivated looking at the old photos of Roger's parents, and the odd photos of his Grandparents and great Aunts and Uncles.

Very few of the photos had names written on the back, but as they went through them, Roger was able to recognise his relatives, and Ginette carefully wrote on the back in pencil. Once this was done, Roger started hunting through for the birth and marriage certificates. To his surprise, not only did he have his parent's, but he also had both sets of Grandparents. Lucy was ecstatic.

"Mum, Dad, this is such a good start. I won't do it tonight just in case I make any silly mistakes, but just looking at them now, there is so much I didn't know about my own relatives. Dad, did you know Nan's maiden name was Herbert? Wasn't it a good job she wasn't a boy they, could have called her Herbert Herbert!"

They all laughed - Lucy's good spirits were contagious. There was a lot of paperwork not really relevant to Lucy's project; old bills, postcards and birthday cards. Roger put them back into the case.

Christine Friend

"Look, Lucy, as you finish with the documents you need, can you put them back. And later on, I think I really do need to go through everything. In actual fact, it would be nice to put the photos in a proper album."
"Of course Dad, no problem. I can work in here tomorrow, instead of moving it around the house. Will that be alright? And then I can't mislay anything."
Ginette was now trying to stifle a yawn, but agreed. "That is a good idea, but perhaps now, if you don't mind, I think I am ready for my bed".


Lucy spent the next two weeks totally engrossed. She had visits from some of her friends, but she didn't feel as left out as she had. By now, she had joined one of the bigger Family History sites, and had ordered numerous birth, marriage and death certificates. Fortunately - as she wasn't being very patient - they were only taking a week to arrive.
In that time, her other grandparents, Ginette's Mum and Dad, popped in frequently and were very encouraging and interested in her finds, but neither seemed to be upset that she wasn't researching their side of the family.

## *Chapter Twenty Eight*

On the Saturday morning, Lucy ,her parents and her Grandparents had all gathered in the large kitchen diner enjoying coffee and fresh apple doughnuts, which her Grandparents had picked up from the local baker. There was a ring at the front door. Roger got up, and made his way into the hall. Their front door was solid oak, but to either side were frosted glass panels. He could see that it was a young man, tall, and it looked as though he was holding a large bunch of flowers. Under his breath, Roger muttered,
"Not Jake, again! Didn't he get the message on his last visit?"
On opening the front door, the young chap turned round. He was about the same height, build, even the same hair colouring as Jake, but he wore glasses, and seemed a bit unsure of himself.
The stranger spoke immediately,
"Hello, does Lucy Wilkinson live here? I was given this address by her friend, Lauren, who is a friend of a friend."
Roger replied,
"Yes, this is her home, and I am her Father, but can I ask..."
Before Roger could finish, the visitor introduced himself as 'Marcus Cummings', he went on to say that he had been the skier who had caused Lucy's fall, and

that he was extremely sorry, and would he pass this message on along with the huge bunch of flowers and an envelope.
Roger was taken aback. The bunch of flowers was the largest Roger had ever seen, and somehow, he seemed so sincere, that Roger actually was starting to feel sorry for him.
"Don't just stand on the doorstep, come in. We are having coffee at the moment, come through and meet Lucy properly."
Roger led the way into the kitchen, and then, hesitantly, introduced Marcus to the family. It was when he noticed the look on his daughter's face, that he began to regret extending this invitation.
Ginette was up out of her chair, and offering Marcus a cup of coffee. But Lucy was silently, glaring at the visitor.
Marcus refused the coffee, and offered the flowers and envelope to Lucy. She took them, but then, in quite an aggressive tone, said,
"How did you find out where I live? And my name? And do you *really* think a bunch of flowers is going to make everything alright?"
The atmosphere in the kitchen changed. Lucy's family were now feeling embarrassed for the young man.
"I tracked you down through a friend of a friend to Lauren. I would have come sooner, but it seemed better to wait until you were a little further along in your recovery. Any sooner, and I was worried I'd just upset you."
"What made you think you wouldn't upset me now?"

"Well, I wasn't sure, but it was a risk I thought I should take."
Ginette spoke,
"Marcus, please, have a cup of coffee, it is still quite cold outside. Have you travelled far?"
"That would be very nice, thank you. I live in Twickenham with my parents at the moment, as I am working locally."
The tension started to ease, and Roger joined in the conversation,
"Twickenham, are you a rugby supporter by any chance?"
The conversation carried on, but Lucy just sat and listened. After an hour, when the coffee was finished, Marcus got up.
"I am very sorry, Lucy, about the accident, but I have put my mobile number in the envelope. I was just wondering if you could let me know how you get on. Thank you for the coffee, and it was very nice to meet you all."
Everyone said goodbye, and Lucy – ungraciously - thanked him for the flowers. With that, he picked up his coat, and Roger showed him out.
Once the front door had been closed, Lucy's Grandmother said,
"Well, that was a difficult thing for a young man to do, Lucy. Whether you are angry with him or not, to find you, and apologise, and bring such a lovely arrangement of flowers... his apology did sound most sincere..."

Lucy looked at her family. She was beginning to feel badly.

"Yes, I suppose it was. Look, in a couple of days, I'll send him a text."

The subject was closed, and Ginette continued the conversation she was having with her parents before Marcus Cummings had appeared.

## *Chapter Twenty Nine*

On Sunday morning, Lucy received a text from Lauren, it read;

Is it safe to ring you?
Have you forgiven me for passing your address on to Marcus?

It made Lucy laugh, she rang Lauren's phone. It was answered immediately.
"Hi Lucy, I know I should have asked you first. The girls all said I should, but I guessed you would have said no. And more importantly, now, you have got to check out YouTube."
Lucy's reply was friendly and curious.
"Yes you should have asked - and why YouTube?"
"Because your accident was filmed, and is on there. Apparently, someone was filming the resort and caught everything. You probably aren't going to like this, but Marcus didn't cause the accident. He was knocked into by someone else, and that caused a domino effect that led to him colliding with you."
Lucy couldn't believe what she was hearing.

"Oh no, that means I will have to apologise to him, I was so rude! Well at least I have a mobile number for him. I think I will just text."
"Lucy, that is a bit cowardly" she said, smirking, "how about offering to meet him for a drink?"
"That's a good idea - and how do you suppose I get there?"
Lauren started to laugh.
"You could always ask your Mum and Dad to take you."
"That makes me sound like a five year old. Thanks Lauren, I'll think about it."
The girls went on to more general chat, and Lucy forgot all about Marcus until later that day.
 Ginette was refreshing the water in the vase of flowers that Marcus had given her, and casually mentioned how nice they were. Lucy told her Mother about Lauren's call.
"Lauren is right, Mum, Marcus isn't to blame. I looked at it myself. So it's my turn to apologise. Lauren suggested that I invite Marcus out for a drink. What do you think?"
Ginette, flattered that she should be asked such a question, agreed. She suggested that, if Lucy liked, she could take her and pick her up later.
Lucy found Marcus's number and texted him.
She didn't mention the accident, but thanked him again for the flowers and asked him if he would like to meet for a drink.
He didn't reply straight away, and Lucy started to feel embarrassed about her behaviour. It was just after 8pm, and Lucy's phone pinged. With relief, she saw it

was Marcus, and that he would look forward to seeing her again, and, although busy, the following week he was free at the weekend, and if she would like, he could drive over and they could go out to lunch. Lucy replied straight away. Yes, that would be great.

Marcus arrived on time. Roger opened the door to him as he had done the week before, but this time, he noticed no signs of trepidation. They went into the kitchen, and again, Lucy's Grandparents were visiting. While Lucy was getting her coat on, Marcus was telling them how lucky it had worked out, him having two Saturday's in a row, off duty. Of course no one knew what Marcus did for a living, and so Ginette, in her naïve way, just asked him.
"Oh, didn't I say, I am a Doctor working in A&E at the West Middlesex. That's why I am living back with my parents. It seems silly not to, as it is only five minutes up the road."
There was no time for anyone to respond. Lucy called from the hall that she was ready. Ginette went to the front door with both of them to wave them goodbye. By the time she was back in the kitchen, there was a general sense of approval of the young man escorting Lucy.

## *Chapter Thirty*

From then on, Lucy's friendship with Marcus developed. Her life, although not back to normal as she was still not back to work, was now busy and full. It was now eight weeks after the accident, and her orthopaedic surgeon at St. Albans General was extremely pleased with her progress. He wanted her to make an appointment two weeks time, and then providing everything was still on target, she could then return to work two weeks later. Lucy was pleased with the news, but this gave her a new urgency to complete more of her Family History.

As prophesied, all went well at Lucy's next appointment, and she was declared fit for work by the physiotherapist.

Life now for Lucy, was even more hectic than before her accident. She enjoyed her job as a P.A to a very busy Solicitor's in the City. After work, there was always someone she could socialise with, either to go out for a meal or a drink. Occasionally, someone in the office would get last minute tickets to see a show. Then there were her girlfriends, who had various jobs working up in town. And on top of that, now she had Marcus in her life. Due to the shifts that he did, and frequently having to be on call, his hours never seemed to follow a pattern. But Lucy made him her priority. In a lot of ways, he was totally different from Jake. He was much kinder and far more understanding, better with money and although he had a serious side, he also had a lovely sense of humour. The likenesses were their looks, being the same height, build and colouring - the only real difference was that Marcus wore glasses. She did ask him once if he had ever considered wearing contacts, but he shuddered and said he couldn't bear the thought of putting something in his own eyes. This made her laugh.

Everyone in Lucy's office was booking annual leave, but after just having had twelve weeks sick leave earlier on in the year, she felt that she should wait and see what was left before booking any time off herself. There was also the question of who she was going to go away with? Her parents and grandparents were all going to Scotland for two weeks. They did ask if she wanted to join them, but she wanted to keep her options open. As yet, she hadn't mentioned holidays to Marcus, she didn't want to frighten him off.

So it happened that everyone she knew were all away on the same weekend, the family in Scotland, and some of her girlfriends in Corfu. They had invited her, but they had booked it back in February, and she wasn't in the right place then to think of holidays. The rest of her girlfriends were all heavily involved with their partners, and Marcus was going to be on duty the whole weekend.

It felt strange having the whole house to herself. Her parents had been away before, that wasn't new, but after spending three months with having someone around the whole time, the house now felt empty, and quiet.

Christine Friend

Her family history research progress was starting to slow down. Her Herbert's had come to a stop. Her four times great grandmother had been widowed for seven years before giving birth to her only child, but had still named her late husband on the birth certificate. This was a shame, because it seemed all her father's other ancestors had very common surnames. She didn't feel completely confident in her searches, and was considering using the services of a professional genealogist, if only to check her research.

There were two good things that had come out of her skiing accident; the first, was meeting Marcus. And the second - she had managed to save a lot of money, and could quite easily afford the fee of a professional.

On the Saturday morning, she had been shopping. She had emptied her laundry basket and washed and ironed everything. Then given her bedroom and en suite a thorough clean and tidy. While she was doing this, she began to think of her maternal grandparents. If she started to research these branches, and then found more problems, she could hire a professional and sort out all her queries in one go. That way she felt it would justify the cost.

While eating her lunch, the feeling of uncertainty started to creep back in. If she waited, there was a chance that her grandparents would have some documentation that she could use, but they were going to be away for another ten days, and that still wouldn't be any good for Granny. The only thing her grandmother had ever spoken about was losing her mother during the blitz, and as a consequence, had no memorabilia. Her grandmother never really spoke about her childhood, and no one asked, as it was all very sad.

As soon as she had finished her lunch, she got her paperwork out. Lucy was very methodical and conscientious in her undertaking of tasks at work, and she carried these qualities into her hobby. Everyone she researched had their own aide-memoire.

Lucy had always had a lovely relationship with her grandmother. In some ways, she felt her own personality was more similar to her's than to her mother. Looking at her paper work, she realised that there was so much she didn't know. Where was Granny born? She did know it was somewhere in east London. Fortunately, she also knew her maiden name, and that was where she started her search.

Margaret Bailey appeared in 1934 in the listings registered in Stepney. Lucy had no need to doubt that this was her grandmother, as her great grandmother's maiden name was listed as 'Pollard'. She remembered when she was very little, watching a comedy programme where there was an actress with the same surname, her Dad had asked her grandmother in a jokey way, were they related. Lucy felt pleased she had remembered this useless bit of information. Her laptop screen gave her the choice to see the original image on the page of the register, so she clicked on to it. This is what brought it to life for her. She liked seeing the Christian names of the previous generations, noticing that some of these names were beginning a resurgence.

On looking at the page, she saw it was in the first quarter of the year. That was good, as Granny's birthday was January. Then further down, Lucy came to the 'Margaret's. There were nine of them, but casting her eye to the next column - mother's maiden name, she found 'Pollard', registered in Stepney. She was just about to close the page when, just under the 'Margaret's, she noticed another Pollard also registered in Stepney. Looking across the page she saw this child's name was Margery. That was a relief, for a minute she thought she could have been ordering the wrong certificate.

Next, she decided to order her grandfather's birth certificate. That was quite straightforward, his full name was, Donald Urquhart Green, and from the moment he started school, he had the nickname of 'Dug'. For confirmation, Lucy checked his Mother's maiden name, Urquhart, perfect. Marriage certificates next, this was much easier when you knew the information. Her grandparents had celebrated their fifty fourth wedding anniversary last September, therefore they were married in 1955.

Lucy put in the relevant information, and it was first result in the options. She was just about to click on the transcript, when her mobile rang. It was Jenny, which was a surprise because she was supposed to be watching cricket with her newly acquired boyfriend. After listening for five minutes Lucy, realised that her research was finished for the day. Jenny and her boyfriend had had a falling out, and Lucy was evidently now required to offer a shoulder to cry on. While listening to Jenny, she quickly clicked on her grandfather's name, and viewed the transcription. 'Donald Urquhart Green married Margery Bailey'. Then she went to the original image, and this only showed the surname of the spouse, Bailey. Yes everything was fine. She scribbled down the District, Volume and page number, which she needed for ordering the certificate. She quickly logged out, and then went on to the Government website for ordering certificates. She filled in the required fields, and ordered the two birth certificates and one marriage. She put in her card details, pressed order, and then was pleased to see that the certificates would be with her by the following Friday. Feeling guilty for not giving Jenny her full attention, she now reclined in her chair, and became immersed in her friend's misery.

On the following Friday afternoon, one of Lucy's colleagues nipped out of the office to see if she could get some cheap last minute theatre tickets. Lucy was up for an evening out, she wouldn't be seeing Marcus until Saturday afternoon. Nicola came back with four tickets for Mama Mia, good seats, all in the same row. Lucy had already seen it, twice, but not for a couple of years, so she made up the group of four girls.
By the time she got home that evening, it had just turned half past eleven. She checked the post, and there were two envelopes for her. She quickly slit them open. No surprises, both her grandparents birth certificates. She hoped the marriage certificate would arrive in the morning post, then she could add all the

details, and order her great grandparents certificates. She left them on the hall table, and went to bed.
As she would be seeing Marcus in the afternoon, she had decided that any shopping she needed, she would have to do after work on the following Monday. That would give her plenty of time today to get ready - it seemed ages since she had seen him.
She woke up late on the Saturday morning. The weather was glorious, and Lucy felt extremely hungry, realising that she had hardly eaten anything the evening before, as by the time she had left the office, there was only enough time to grab a sandwich and a drink in their local pub, before jumping on the underground to the theatre.
Lucy liked being in the kitchen, and cooked herself toasted avocado on sourdough, with poached eggs and grilled tomato, a small pot of tea, and an apple to finish. By now it was eleven o'clock, and Marcus was aiming to be at her home for two o'clock, so she still had enough time to have a bath, wash her hair and paint her nails. It was only when she came downstairs, all ready to go, did she see the third envelope that she had been waiting for. As she bent down to pick it up off the mat, she heard Marcus's car pull on to the drive. She picked up all three envelopes, and slipped them into her large handbag.
She hurried out the front door, locked it behind her, and ran to his car, jumping in and leaning across to give him a big hello kiss. He seemed a little bashful, which made her laugh, and again mentioned that, for a Doctor he was quite shy. They hadn't made any plans,

but Marcus had asked his mum to put a picnic together for them. This was on the back seat in a very upmarket picnic basket. It didn't take them long to decide where to go, and Lucy gave directions. Thirty minutes later, Marcus was driving into a car park at Broxbourne. Lucy unfolded a picnic blanket under an old beech tree, which was a couple of feet away from the river's edge. For a very slim girl, Lucy had a healthy appetite. And between them, they almost ate everything that was packed into the basket. The weather was just as glorious as it had been that morning, and they both stretched out on the blanket, finding it difficult not to fall asleep, whilst they watched the ducks and swans on the river. The silence between them wasn't embarrassing, just very companionable.

Lucy opened her eyes, and couldn't immediately work out where she was. Then, looking to her right, she saw the gentle movement of Marcus's chest, as he too had fallen asleep. She didn't like to move, all too aware that he had worked many hours the previous week. When she looked at her watch, it was 10 minutes to five. Marcus slept on for another thirty minutes.

It made her laugh when he woke up with a start, as some children had run past playing tag rather excitedly. For a minute, he too couldn't remember where he was, and then a big smile spread across his face.

"How long was I asleep for? Sorry, you must have been bored. You should have woken me up."

"You must have needed the sleep, and don't worry, I nodded off as well."

Marcus looked at his watch,

"What would you like to do, we could stretch our legs and go for a walk, and then perhaps I'll drive us to your home and then take you out for some supper?"
"Actually, a walk sounds just the thing. Shall we finish the coffee first, and I will make us some supper when we get back?"
Feeling more refreshed after the coffee, they walked and talked. By now, it was nearly seven o'clock, but still very hot. They made their way to the car, and Marcus drove them back.
It was only when Lucy opened her handbag to get her front door keys out, that she realised she hadn't opened her third envelope. Not to worry, she decided to open it after they had eaten.
Having had a late lunch, neither of them were too hungry, so Lucy made them a cheese omelette with salad, and poured them a glass of chilled white wine. After they'd had eaten and Lucy had loaded the dishwasher, she made coffee, and they took it out on to the patio. It was still very warm, and Lucy suddenly remembered her certificates. She didn't know if Marcus would find this boring. After all, she wasn't so sure if she would be interested in anyone else's family history? If he was bored, he showed no sign of it, and so she went to get her envelopes. She showed him the two birth certificates first, and explained that 'Urquhart' was her grandfather's mother's maiden name. She also told him that he was known as 'Dug' by so many people, that when he played golf, they put 'Dug' in brackets after his Christian name so that it

cleared any misunderstandings up about who they were playing.

She then slit open the marriage certificate, and read the names.

"Oh, how disappointing, how did I do that? I have ordered the wrong one. Look, it's a 'Margery', instead of 'Margaret Bailey' but, that's strange, it's got Grandad's name on it... *and* the date is right?"

Marcus was very intrigued now.

"Well could it just be the wrong Christian name written into the records? Margery and Margaret are very similar."

Lucy was thinking, and then she suddenly jumped up, remembering,

"There was a 'Margery Bailey' registered at the same time as Granny's birth, and the Mother's maiden name was 'Pollard', the registration district was Stepney, all the same as Granny's. Wait a minute, I'll go and get my Laptop."

When she came back, Marcus was holding Margaret's birth certificate.

"Lucy, has your Grandmother ever told you that she is a twin?"

"No, why, what makes you think that she is?"

"Well I have just noticed, looking at it again, that the time of birth is on the certificate. The time is recorded on to the certificate when there is a multiple birth in case there are any questions over inheritance, as in a title. In such a case, it's necessary to know who is the elder."

Lucy sat down. Marcus could see she was quite shocked. He went to the kitchen, and brought back two glasses of water, and handed one to Lucy. She drank some, then handed the glass back.
"Marcus, I don't understand. If that is the case, then who is my Grandmother? Let me see if there is a death certificate for Margery Green, and a marriage certificate for Gramps to Granny."
Lucy and Marcus spent the rest of the evening on her family history site trying to find the certificates for both these events, but their search came up blank. Lucy was beginning to wish she hadn't started this hobby. Neither she, nor Marcus, could come up with a rational answer. She knew the only way to sort out the problem was to ask her grandparents but she didn't feel she had the right to do this. Marcus could see how tired and upset she was, and suggested that they call it a day.

On Sunday, Marcus drove Lucy to his parent's house for lunch. He glanced at her as he was driving, and thought how very attractive she was, but that she had lost her usual glow this morning.
"Lucy, you have been so quiet this morning, it's not us, is it?
She glanced up at him, and then smiled.
"Of course it's not us. My grandparents will be home tomorrow, and I really don't know if I can face them. How can I question them? I am trying not to think of it, I don't want it to spoil today. Your Mum always goes to so much trouble."

The couple both fell silent, and then suddenly Lucy spoke,
"That's it, I have just decided what I am going to do. I am going to talk to Granny when she is on her own. When I go into the office tomorrow, I can rearrange my schedule so that I can take Wednesday off. I will go and see Granny in the morning. She is always in Wednesday morning. She goes to the hairdressers in the afternoon, all ready for lunch out with the girls on Thursday. And Grandad is always out playing golf Wednesday morning with the seniors. Yes, I have decided. That's what I'll do."
Marcus added,
"Just remember that whatever the reason is, even if you don't think it is right, they will feel they did it for the best."
"Yes, I know. I feel so much better having a plan. Come on Marcus step on it. I feel absolutely famished now. Not eating any breakfast wasn't a good idea."

## *Chapter Thirty One*

Lucy left for the office early. She wanted to be at her desk, at the latest, for 8 o'clock. That way, it would give her a chance of clearing as much work as she could. If that wasn't enough, then she would stay late. Her parents were arriving home Monday afternoon. She didn't really want to spend much time with them before Wednesday. She thought her face would give her away, and her Dad was sure to ask how she was getting on. He seemed to take a real interest in her research.
In the end, she did stay late. She did the same on the Tuesday, an early start and late finish. What was at the back of Lucy's mind was that, if things went badly with her granny on Wednesday, she might not feel up to going to work on Thursday. But if she could get all her work done before hand, she wouldn't be letting anyone down, and certainly not Mr Crawford, whom she worked for.

Marcus sent Lucy a text early Wednesday morning, and to her delight, he had managed to be free that evening and would be over to see her. The thought of him being so supportive gave Lucy confidence, in what was a difficult situation. After all, this was her grandparent's business, what if it changed the lovely relationship she had with them? The only other option was to say nothing, but they were no one's fools, and would surely wonder why she hadn't shown any interest in their family history.

Lucy was up early. She showered, and washed her hair. She chose to wear one of her new dresses she had bought for the summer. A sleeveless, fitted, and full skirted retro dress. It was in a bold red and white pattern, and her glossy, shiny brown curly hair was tied back in a high pony tail.

When she came down to breakfast, Ginette and Roger both looked at their stunning daughter with pride. Ginette was intrigued.

"Lucy you look lovely, are you going to work? It seems a shame you aren't seeing Marcus when you're looking so nice."

Lucy replied while buttering some toast,

"I am seeing Marcus later. I thought that I should start using some annual leave, and Monday and Tuesday were so busy in the office, I asked Mr Crawford for today off. I found out that some of the libraries with reference departments have family history sites, so my plan is to visit them."

Roger was nodding his head with approval.

"I must say Lucy, you really have got the bug. Do you want a lift, I don't have to leave so early today?"

"Thanks, Dad, but I thought I would drive. I might pop in on Granny first. I haven't seen them since you all got back."

At quarter past nine, Lucy left for her Grandparents house, giving the school run mums a chance to be off the road. Maggie and Donald only lived a five minute drive away, but past two schools.

Pulling on to the gravel drive, she could see her grandad's car was missing. That was a relief, she didn't feel that she had the confidence to face them both. She hurriedly locked her car and walked to the front door. Her Grandparents house was a large five bedroom detached house, built in the 1930's. It had originally been built as a four bedroom house, but over the years they had tastefully extended it to include three en-suites, a massive kitchen, a conservatory, and an extra bedroom with dressing room.

Lucy rang the doorbell and her granny came and opened the front door. The expression on Maggie's face as she saw Lucy standing there was one of delight. "Lucy, how lovely! come in. Excellent timing, I now have an excuse to put the coffee on."

By now, Maggie had walked half way up the hall. The hall way was tiled in a Victorian, old English style, in black and white, and it was impossible to walk on it in shoes without making a noise. Maggie stopped, she realised Lucy wasn't following her. She turned to see Lucy having walked through the front door, but standing still on the door mat. Maggie walked back towards her and realised that Lucy was silently crying. Maggie was still striking to look at, and at 76, was still 5 foot 9 inches tall, and so was able to wrap her arms around her granddaughter. She very quietly spoke.

"Lucy, you know don't you."

And Lucy whispered back.

"Granny - I know something - but I don't know what."

Maggie took Lucy by the hand, and led her through the lounge to a doorway on the sidewall. This opened up into the conservatory, which by definition, was used as a sun lounge, and was where Maggie grew her delicate plants and her collection of orchids. As with the rest of the house, the décor and furnishings were lovely, Maggie had impeccable taste.
They sat together on one of the cane settees, facing one another. Then Maggie spoke,
"Your Grandfather and I have always thought that, at some stage, I would have to break a promise. The promise was made on condition that it could be broken only If an explanation was really necessary. I think looking at your face, that time is here. It wouldn't be fair for you to know everything at this moment, because in doing so, you would then carry the burden of a secret from your Mother. If it is OK with you, I will explain what you have discovered. Then today, I will invite your mum and dad, uncle Mike and yourself, and you will know everything. That's, if you want to?"
"I am so sorry Granny. It's my fault, I should have asked you and Gramps first before delving into your past."
Maggie's voice, which had been normal, instantly became quite censorious,
"It is not your fault. Never ever think that. Had it been a problem, then we would have said so when you told us of your new hobby. You see, I am actually pleased we can tell you all now. My fear was that, one day when Grandad and I had gone someone would have uncovered something and needed answers, and it

would all be too late. Let me make some coffee, and then you can tell me everything you know."
Five minutes later, Maggie was back with a cafetière, milk, sugar, cups, saucers and a chocolate cake. Lucy had just returned from the cloakroom, as she felt the need to refresh herself with some cold water on her face, and hopefully erase the blotches from her cheeks. Maggie poured the coffee, cut the cake, and asked Lucy to tell her what she knew.
Lucy now felt far more composed, and reached in her bag for the three certificates.
"When you were away, I thought I would start on your side of the family. I knew yours and Gramp's mother's maiden names, so finding your birth certificates was easy. Then when I was looking for your marriage certificate, I was distracted with a phone call from Jenny and didn't realise that it was for a Donald and Margery until it arrived on Saturday. Marcus was with me when I opened it, and he said that perhaps the wrong name had been recorded, but I remembered that when I found your birth certificate I noticed below that there was a Margery. Her Mother's maiden name was Pollard, and she was also registered in Stepney. Then, yesterday, I was having my lunch at my desk in the P.A office with Maria and Louise, and I remembered something else. It was Maria who actually made me remember. She was talking about her new diet and was moaning about no butter and bread, which are her two favourite things. Beryl the senior P.A. walked in and said that perhaps she should try margarine? Well that made me remember what

Mum once told me when I was about eight. She said that when she was little, she could never remember whether your name was Margery or margarine, because when she was very little people called you 'Marg'. Oh, there is something else. When Marcus looked at your birth certificate, he seemed to think you were a twin, because your time of birth is recorded on there."

"Yes, Marcus is absolutely right. I was – am - a twin. Margery and I were completely identical; looks, height, even voice. When we went to grammar school, for fun, we would take it in turns to speak and our friends would have their eyes closed, and they would try and guess who it was talking. I say 'guess', because that was all they *could* do, as we were so identical. By now, you will have realised that Grandad was married to Margery, so there is no mistake on the certificate."

"I know it sounds silly to ask, but you did say you were totally identical... Gramp's knows you are not Margery, doesn't he?"

For the first time since Lucy had arrived, Maggie laughed and so did she, which at once put them both at ease.

"Yes, Grandad knows. Lucy, I wish I could tell you so much more, but all I can really say is that it was Margery that instigated this situation, and I have to add, no foul play was involved."

They both laughed again. Lucy felt more herself.

"If I thought there was, I wouldn't have come to see you."

"While you are here, let's get this all sorted as soon as possible. I am going to phone your mum and uncle Mike."
Maggie went back into the lounge, and picked up the phone. She came back and sat down.
"Let me try Mike first, he is always a nightmare to pin down."
She dialled his dental practice number, and very promptly, the phone was answered. Maggie asked to be put through to Mike and waited while the phone rang. Another young female voice answered and Maggie repeated her request and this time told the dental nurse that it was important. Mike came to the phone.
"Hello Mother, everything OK? You and Dad are alright?"
"Yes, Mike, we are completely well, but we do need to see you on some rather important family business - are you free this Saturday? Come to lunch, and then we can talk after."
"Well actually, Saturday would suit me fine and I can introduce my new girlfriend to you."
"Sorry Michael, this visit is for family only I am afraid. That visit will have to be another day. I will phone Ginette, now if you don't hear from me again today then your Father and I will see you Saturday, 12 o'clock."
"This all sounds a bit mysterious. No worries, I will be there. Got to dash, got a patient in the chair, bye."
And he hung up.
Maggie, talking as much to herself as to Lucy, said,

"Can he introduce his new girlfriend? He has so many girlfriends, is it likely to be a different one by Saturday!"
While talking, she was dialling her daughter's number. It rang a few times, and then it was picked up.
"Hello, Ginette, Mum here. Are you and Roger free on Saturday for lunch? There is something Dad and I want to talk to you about."
"Oh no, you are not going in to a home?"
Maggie replied most indignantly.
"Certainly not, Mike will be here and I have already checked with Lucy."
"That will be lovely, let's hope the weather doesn't change, then we will all be able to sit out in the garden."
"Yes, exactly, see you then."
Maggie hung up. She looked at Lucy,
"That's it. Now let's have a walk round the garden, and forget about it all until Saturday. Are you OK with that?"
"Completely. Let's make the most of my day off."

That evening, Marcus arrived at Lucy's parents for dinner. Lucy saw him arrive out of the lounge window. He was wearing navy tailored shorts, and a long sleeve white shirt with the sleeves turned back, and the neck open. He had sunglasses on, and tan suede loafers on his feet. For the first time since she had met him, she got butterflies in her stomach. She ran to the front door, and before he could even say 'hello', she had thrown her arms around him.

After dinner, Lucy and Marcus went out for a drive, and ten minutes later came across a quaint old pub advertising a beer garden. Soon they were sitting with their drinks, and it was then that Marcus asked her how her visit to Maggie's went.

"It is going to sound very strange, but I actually think she was pleased. Apparently, Margery, who was her identical twin sister, made her promise not to tell anyone, unless, something had been discovered and it was necessary. She said that both Gramp's and herself have felt guilty about the lie."

"Have you told your Mum and Dad?"

"No, while I was there, Granny phoned Mum and Uncle Mike. The four of us are going to lunch on Saturday. She didn't tell them why. Just that there is some family business that needs discussing. I am sorry, it's your first weekend off for ages."

"No worries, Dad's friend who goes to the rugby with him is away, so I'll go and have his ticket. Dad will like that, but we are still good for Sunday?"

"Yes, of course. How do you think my Mum and Uncle are going to take the news, whatever it is?"

"Be optimistic about it. Your Grandparents are very nice people. I think a nice day out on Sunday will give you something to look forward to."

## *Chapter Thirty Two*

Saturday proved to be another scorching hot day. Lucy noticed her Father was rather quiet, but her Mother chatted away as though there couldn't possibly be any kind of problem looming. At 12 o'clock, the three of them were ready to leave. Lucy had popped out earlier and bought some flowers for them to take, and Roger had picked a rather good bottle of white wine.
As they pulled on to the drive Michael, pulled in behind them, driving another new car. This time it was a Morgan. Roger walked over to have a look. Michael jumped out, pleased to show off his new acquisition. There was no breeze, and the temperature was already at 28 degrees. Ginette and Lucy made their way to the front door. Ginette knocked, and they could hear Maggie's heels tapping on the floor tiles as she came to open the door.
Giving Maggie a kiss, Ginette said,
"Hello Mum. Look at Roger and Mike - toys for the boys."
She didn't seem to notice her Mother and how she looked, but Lucy did. In fact, Lucy was quite shocked by her Grandmother's appearance. She was beautifully dressed, her hair and makeup immaculate, but her face was very drawn and tired. Lucy saw bags under her grandmother's eyes. She kissed her on the cheek, and was now fighting hard not to show any emotion. This was her fault, she had caused this stress and anxiety

that her Grandmother was going through. She handed her the flowers, and for the first time ever as they looked at each other, the bond of love was felt totally by both of them.

Maggie called to her son and son-in-law to come in. Like naughty boys, they obeyed, but continued to talk about Mike's car.

The lunch was as delicious as it was simple. They started with melon and Parma ham. Main course was crab and langoustine salad, served with new potatoes and small crusty rolls. Dessert, was Eton Mess followed by a cheese board. Lucy noticed that Maggie hardly ate anything but by time the cheese and biscuits were on the table, Donald had regained his appetite. Strangely, but unmentioned by all, was that no wine or any other alcoholic drink was offered, and so everyone drank only chilled water. The conversation was light hearted, and Mike was allowed to take centre stage by telling funny stories about his numerous patients.

Once the lunch was over, Maggie seemed in a hurry to move onto coffee, in the lounge. The ladies cleared the table and loaded the dishwasher, and the three men went into the lounge, where it was pleasantly cool, a gentle breeze blowing through the open windows. Mike attracted Roger's attention, and was discretely trying to find out if he knew why they had all been summoned. Roger shrugged his shoulders and shook his head. The two men realised that there was now a certain tension in the room. They looked across at Donald, who seemed to be staring off into space.

When Life Changes Direction

The three ladies came into the lounge together, all carrying various items for the coffee. No sooner had they all sat down, Maggie started to speak.
"Your Father and I have something of great importance to tell you all. We would rather you have known this many years ago." Looking to Ginette and Mike she said, "I wished I could have told you this when you were children, but I had made a promise, and it would have meant breaking it. The circumstances have now changed, and because of that it, enables me to legitimately break that promise. Your Father and I realise that you will probably have a lot of questions, and may even be very angry, and we are truly sorry, but we hope you will understand why we are only telling you now"
Lucy looked around the room. Her grandfather was nodding at everything her grandmother said. Uncle Mike was seemingly, half paying attention, as he always looked as though his mind was on other things - usually - his current girlfriend. Her mother was listening, but also in a very distracted way, and her Father was perched on the edge of the sofa. Before Maggie continued, she asked Donald if he could get her a glass of water. Donald jumped out of his seat, and within seconds was handing the glass to his wife. She took a sip. Placed the glass on the coffee table and continued,
"The person that asked me to keep this secret, was my identical twin sister Margery. I know I have never spoken of her before, but there is a reason. We were completely identical, even our voices, the only person

who could really tell us apart was our mother. In April, 1960, I was running my own business. It had been left to me by my beloved friend Penelope, who really treated me like a daughter and who I looked upon as my surrogate Mother"

"Mum, what kind of business?" Mike interrupted. Maggie was surprised, it was though he had woken from a trance. She replied, "It was two, ladies dress shops, both up in town. South Kensington and Chelsea. We had wealthy customers, and could make alterations on the premises. It wasn't couture, but it wasn't off the peg either. They were limited designs that we had made to measure."

Mike interrupted again.

"What kind of turn over did you have?"

Maggie snapped, "Michael do you mind! I am trying to tell you something of huge importance. Please don't interrupt again. Once I have finished you may ask anything you wish."

By calling her son 'Michael', she let him know how annoyed she was. As a child, he was known as 'Mikey', unless he was in trouble. Only then was his full name used. She continued,

"On this particular day, I received a call from my sister. By now we were not close. We hadn't seen or heard from each other in over five years. She desperately wanted to meet me, and suggested I go to see her in a nursing home in Kings Langley. I went home from work at lunchtime, and then drove to the home in the afternoon. It was a private nursing home. It was in its own grounds, and looked amazing, like a property from

a period drama. It was cheery, and very comfortable. On my arrival, one of the staff took me into the gardens where Margery was sitting waiting for me. She didn't say anything on the phone about her appearance, and I was very shocked. She had lost so much weight, there was nothing of her. Her hair was thin and had lost its shine, and her face was sunken". Maggie turned to Donald.
"I am so sorry dear, would you rather go out?"
Everyone turned to look at Donald. He looked extremely sad. He didn't speak, he just nodded his head for Maggie to continue.
"We sat and talked, I don't know what about, I was still so shaken. After the pleasantries, she asked if I minded going back to her room - she wanted to speak in confidence. She could see my concern about her walking, so suggested that I go and find a nurse who would help. I did just that. The nurse brought a wheelchair, and as we were walking back, she told me how glad the medical staff were that I had come to visit, that I was her first visitor, and as her next of kin, it was important that I was there. I was a bit surprised to hear I was her next of kin, because when she phoned, she had called herself 'Mrs Green'."
Maggie leant forward, picked up her glass of water, and sipped some more. She seemed to compose herself, and then carried on.
"We went to her room, which was very nice. The nurse said she would order us some tea and cakes. The tea, with little finger sandwiches and cakes, arrived on a trolley. The nurse who bought it in said to Margery that

she hoped she would try and eat something, and looked at me for some support.
It was only after she left, did Margery start to tell me why she had phoned. She had come over from Germany where she lived with her husband and two children, a little girl, four years old, and a baby boy of eighteen months. She had undergone a hysterectomy here in England, but she had left it too late, and they had told her that her life expectancy was no longer than two to three months. She had come to terms with that, but she needed to leave her family in good hands. That was where I came in. She wanted me to take over. I thought she meant that I should take on my role as Aunt. But no, she wanted me to literally take her place. We were absolutely identical, no one would know. There is no easy way to say this - I am not Margery, but Margaret. Ginette, Mike, I am your Aunt, not your Mother."
There was total silence. Maggie and Donald looked at each other. Maggie was becoming agitated, she was expecting some kind of reaction - even if it was anger.
"Ginette, Mike, did you hear what I said? I am not your Mother. I am your Aunt."
Ginette looked up,
"Sorry Mum, I was listening, but I am not sure what you want me to say. You are my Mother. You brought me up. I was only four. I do vaguely remember you coming back from England, and you seemed to me to have a lot of new clothes and shoes, but I don't really recall much else. You still looked the same. No, your hair was a bit different. It was shorter and, yes, you

smelt of a lovely flowery smell, but other than that nothing had changed."

"But Ginette, I wasn't your Mother. And I have been deceitful."

Maggie was starting to feel agitated, the significance of her statement seemingly being ignored.

"Yes, I do understand that. But as you say, you were identical twins, doesn't that mean that you both came from the same egg? So really, you are the other half of Margery."

Everyone was now listening to Ginette, she was probably the least logical person anyone could wish to meet and yet, what she said seemed very logical.

Mike now joined in,

"Mum, I was only a baby. You were my Mum. I have absolutely no memory of anyone else. I agree with Ginny. I may not put it in quite the same way, but it makes sense. It doesn't change anything. It's like you adopted us and didn't tell us. You are our Mother."

Lucy couldn't believe what she was seeing. Mike got up, and went and kissed Maggie on the cheek. Maggie burst into tears. He knelt, and took her in his arms. How long this tableau lasted for, she had no idea but it was very moving.

Maggie gained control, and Mike stood and went and sat back on the sofa.

Ginette started to speak and everyone turned to face her,

"What happened never affected me, and I can't see that it ever will. You are saying you didn't have any choice, that is good enough for me. I think at the moment, you two are the one's struggling with what happened. If it helps you both to tell us more, then do, but don't do it for me. I don't need, or want, to know any more."

Donald, who had not yet spoken, turned to Mike, and asked how he felt.

"Dad, I feel the same as Ginny. You and Mum gave me a brilliant childhood. I don't want to see either of you upset, but if there is anything else to be said that would help you both, we do want to be supportive."

He stopped speaking, it was still quiet, so he continued,

"What I don't get is, why Margery didn't want anybody to know?"

Donald took up the story.

"Margery was a very private, and shy person. We met while she was working in York university library for post grad students. I was lucky enough to have access, and she was extremely helpful ordering material I needed for my job, which was working in Germany as a civil servant. Being fluent in German was a great asset. My parents knew Mr and Mrs Barnes through the church in Harrogate. They were the couple whom Margery and Mum had been evacuated to, from Stepney, East London. Mr and Mrs Barnes had lived here in St. Albans before moving to Harrogate. My parents used to do fund raising for the church and one Sunday afternoon, in the summer of 1954, they organised a garden party and Margery arrived with, well, she called them 'Aunt Edith' and 'Uncle Edward' and I said Hello and, 'what a coincidence' as we had already met. Well, my parents instantly thought she was the girl for me, and I think so did Edith and Edward. At that time I would be home one weekend in four from Germany, and it all fell into place. I proposed to her just after her 21$^{st}$ birthday, in the January. She accepted, and we married in the September. Ginette was born the following year. Just after we married, Edward died, and we asked Edith to come and live in Germany with us. We had a good life. Margery always had an au pair. There was a good social scene, we both thought Edith would like it, and I thought it would help Margery. You see, her shyness held her back in life. In the end, Edith decided she wanted to stay in Harrogate, and she died not long after Ginette was born. I do feel a sense of guilt as, looking back, I can see now that she wasn't happy. She didn't really mix with the other wives, and it was probably harder as she was so young. Margery and me didn't have a good physical relationship, and it took us both by surprise when she fell pregnant with you, Mike. She seemed to blossom though while she was pregnant, but then not long after you were born, she seemed to retreat back into herself again. I had had a number of promotions..."

With this, Donald put his head in his hands. Mike, being compassionate for the second time that day, told his father that he didn't have to say any more, but Donald shook his head.

"I must finish, because if I don't tell you this, you won't be able to understand how Margery was ill and was able to hide it from me. By time you were six months old, Mike, our relationship was no longer husband and wife, but more, brother and sister. One of my colleagues, a kind chap, could see that I was unhappy, and let me confide in him about my life with Margery. He told me he had gone through a similar situation, and that in time, once the children were no longer babies, life would sort itself out. Whether I really believed him, or I told myself it was true because I wanted it to be, I don't know. But either way, I just stepped back, and hoped for things to get better. It was just after New Year, 1960, and Margery went to see a Gynaecologist. She wouldn't let me go with her. Looking back, I should have insisted. The outcome was that she needed to have a hysterectomy. She didn't want to have it in Germany, so it was decided that she would go back to England. The original plan was for us both to fly back, and I would be over here for her first week, then on her second week she would transfer to a nursing home. A couple of days before we were due to leave, she changed her mind, and instead, I flew over the second week but stayed only a couple of days. She kept saying that she hated me seeing her looking so awful, and that as soon as she had recovered fully she would fly back to Germany, but until then, she would be better on her own. I was a coward. I don't know why, but I took the easy option. We had one au pair and a nanny looking after you both, and they were doing an excellent job. Ginette was going to a kindergarten, and you were both settled and well. When Margery moved to the nursing home, she would phone almost every day. If I asked for the address she

would get upset, and accuse me of not trusting her. Looking back, it was all wrong, but I was a young man. After getting to her know her Aunt Edith, I put it down to a repressed childhood, and just looked forward to her recovery and return. Then one day, she told me that she had met up with an old school friend, and was going to go to Scotland with her for a couple of weeks, and then she'd come home. She said it would be difficult to phone, and that she loved me and the children."
Everyone in the room looked shocked as Donald started to cry.
Mike, Ginette, Roger and Lucy left the room, while Maggie sat with her husband. They could hear her telling him,
"It's alright, Donald it's all over."
The four of them went into the kitchen. Lucy put the kettle on, and Roger started getting the bits and pieces needed to make some tea. Mike looked up at the clock.
"Crikey, it's 6pm. I am supposed to be meeting Liz at 7pm, I'll never make it now. I'll go outside and let her know it isn't going to happen".
With that he went into the garden. Ginette raised her eyebrows.
"Well, I never thought he would put Mum and Dad before a new girlfriend. It's serious, isn't it"
Roger answered,
"Mum and Dad, or the Girlfriend?"
"Both" was Ginette's reply.
Lucy was looking in the fridge.

"Look Mum, there is some cold meat, cheese and other nibbles. Should we make some sandwiches and put the pickles and cheese out? what do you think?"
Before she could answer, a voice came from the door way,
"That's a very good idea Lucy."
It was Maggie, and she was now back in control.
"Let's set it up in the dining room. A change of scenery will be nice, and perhaps if we all have something to eat, it will give your father and me a break, and take the pressure off."
It was just then that she realised Mike was missing.
"Has Mike gone?"
"No Mum, he is in the garden. He is on the phone to Liz. Don't worry, it is family first today for all of us."
The table was set in the dining room and Donald asked if anyone would like a glass of something. The three ladies opted for white wine. Donald, Mike and Roger all had whisky and soda. Mike had already checked with Maggie as to him staying over, as he actually felt he needed a drink.
While they were eating, Maggie carried on with the story,
"Even identical twins can differ in personality. As Dad said, Margery was much more private than myself. I think that was why Edith preferred Margery to me. It was sad that we had become so distant, but I always thought that Edith had manipulated the situation. Penelope invited Margery and myself to go travelling with her for two weeks to France and Italy. Remember, people didn't have holidays abroad then, and I couldn't

wait, but Margery turned the offer down. Edith used this to plan a strategy to separate us. We discovered on our return that the three of them had moved to Harrogate. If Margery had had a stronger personality, then she would have stood up to Edith. She might have even put up more of a fight with the cancer. I am afraid when she first told me her prognosis, I wasn't very kind".

Although they were all still eating, Maggie had now their full attention.

"You see, in that first visit, Margery let it slip that she knew I was unable to have any children of my own. In the May after our 21$^{st}$ birthday, I had an emergency operation to save my life, I had peritonitis. The infection had spread, and the only option was to perform a hysterectomy at the same time. Well Margery knew all that, and yet she had made no contact to see how I was, and how I was coping with the operation - and losing my beloved Penelope. As I said earlier, Penelope became my surrogate mother. I had been rushed into Hospital and Connie, Penelope's housekeeper, contacted her to let her know. Penelope left work and got the first train home. She was so worried for me, that…"

Maggie was finding it hard to speak, she was clearly getting distressed. Mike interrupted,

"Mum, you don't need to tell us if it is too painful for you."

"Thank you dear, but I must. I want you to understand my motives. Penelope was so worried for me that she ran out of St.Albans station trying to get a taxi, and was hit by a car. She was killed instantly. Now, Margery knew all this. I was so angry with her that I picked up my handbag and walked out of her room. I could hear her calling me back, and apologising and crying, but I didn't want to see her. Or help her.

I didn't tell anybody of our meeting. Not even Connie, who lived with me in this house. Then a couple of days later, I came home from work and there was a letter waiting for me. I didn't recognise the writing. It was from Margery, it was poorly written, and it had obviously been a struggle for her. In it, she apologised, and said that Connie had written to Edith, and that Edith had thought it a bad idea for her to contact me about her wedding. Edith said it would spoil Margery's wedding having me there in my sad state, and recovering from surgery. Margery knew even then, that she should not have agreed, and there was no excuse. She explained that if she could, she would do it all differently now. That was why she wanted to give me her children, to try and make amends. And she knew she could trust me with the most precious things in her life.

Connie knew something big was wrong, and I felt bad not confiding in her, but Margery had made me promise not to discuss it with anyone. On the following Saturday, I went back to the nursing home, and again the staff were clearly very pleased to see me. Margery had lost even more weight, but was genuinely relieved, and happy that I was back. It was then that she told me her plan. I listened and asked questions. I never lost my temper, or stormed out again. We were back as one, we were twins – identical."

"Granny, can I ask, when did you first meet Gramps?"

"This seems outrageous now, but I didn't meet Grandad until after Margery had died. Margery thought the only way I could step into her life was if it was done in secrecy. The only phone number and address she gave me, was that of her Solicitor. I immediately contacted him, and he told me that he had clear instructions as to the details of her funeral, and only after, was he able to pass on a letter which would contain valuable information for me. I tried to talk Margery round, but she was insistent, so I had a choice; a husband and children, or my business, and the knowledge that I'd abandoned my sister in her hour of need. So I made my choice. I had decided years before, after I'd had my operation, that there was no point in my ever getting married. I felt I may as well keep my independence, and enjoy myself, having no commitments. But suddenly everything changed for me. The next few weeks, as Margery got weaker, I visited every day. She would tell me about her life; her husband, children, your father's colleagues and any other useful bits of information. Before she had actually made contact with me, she had written me notes, so I studied these and she would question me."

Maggie looked around the table before she continued, "My biggest worry was meeting your Father. What if I really didn't like him? What kind of life was I expected to live? What kind of marriage? I asked Margery this. Believe me, it wasn't an easy conversation. All she would say was that she had never liked that side of marriage, and so the ball was in my court."

There was a strangled laugh. It was Mike. He went very red.

"Sorry Mum, I didn't mean anything by that, it just sounded like a funny phrase to use in the circumstances."

It was now just after 9pm. Donald asked if they should perhaps stop, but the general feeling was that as long as Maggie was alright then she should carry on.

So Maggie continued.

"Margery didn't live for very much longer. She did tell me that, had she not been so prudish, she would have seen a Doctor a lot earlier. She knew a few months after Mike had been born that things were not right, but she was too shy, embarrassed, to seek help. Then when the situation became impossible to live with, she visited the Gynaecologist. She said it didn't take her long before she had made her plan, which was why she was insistent on having her treatment back in England. As Dad said, she phoned almost every day. She told Dad about the trip to Scotland because she knew she was near to dying. I think she gave up towards the end. She was on a lot of morphine, and I think she was tired of everything. I was with her. It was so very sad. After she passed away, I told Connie, and she let Edna, Edith's old housekeeper, know. And so there were three of us, plus the Solicitor, at her funeral. She was buried in St.Albans Green Park cemetery. Neither Connie, or Edna asked any questions as to why no one else was there. Before Margery and Dad had married,

Edna had left Edith's employment and went and lived with her older sister. She didn't like living in Harrogate. Edith, apparently, was very annoyed, and so Edna lost contact with them, but she still remained friends with Connie."

Maggie composed herself.

"I thought that perhaps, soon, I could take you to the cemetery. She was very thorough with the funeral details. She ordered her own headstone, and left explicit instructions as to what had to be engraved. You see, she was buried under her maiden name, and she had also booked into the nursing home as Margery Bailey. I think that was the name on her death certificate as well. I'm not sure, it's a long time since I've looked at it, but she was so sure that I would agree and take her place."

Lucy realised this was why she had been unable to find Margery's death certificate, and was restraining herself from shedding a tear.

Maggie carried on talking. Her family listened.

She told them how understanding the Solicitor was.

"Margery had said, if only to start with, I would have to curb my enthusiasm for things and read a bit more. There was, of course, my business, and Margery wanted me to sell it as soon as possible, but I told her that wasn't up for discussion. I would sell it providing everything went well, but I felt I needed to keep it as a safety net just in case. My house, this house, was also not included in Margery's plan. I couldn't sell it. It had been Penelope's. Your father mentioned Margery and I having been evacuated from Stepney to St. Albans, well Edith and Edward's house that we lived in is next door to us here, number 40. Ruth and Martin's." No one even gasped in surprise, so much had already been revealed.

Maggie told them that not all her visits to Margery were about 'the plan'. Sometimes they talked about their childhood. On one such visit, Margery told Maggie about their father's disappointment over them not being boys. The twins had only just started school, but on this particular day, Margery had woken up feeling unwell. Tommy happened to be on leave, and was annoyed that one of his daughters was at home. When he was on leave, he tended to be quite possessive of his wife. Margery was in the front room, and she could hear her father arguing with her mother. Tommy shouted that, had they been boys, he wouldn't have allowed them to be babied. He would have spent more time with them himself. Agnes retorted by saying that he spent such little time with them, that he couldn't even tell them apart. Tommy laughed at this, a cruel laugh, then said that it didn't matter, his mate who he had met the day he registered them had the right idea. Hadn't Agnes realised that he always called them both 'Marg' - short for Margaret, *and* Margery? That way, he didn't have to bother to work out which one was which. Now Agnes was crying out. "How could you! how can you even call yourself a father? You knew that it had meant a lot to me to call them Isabel and Daisy."

Margery heard their father walk past the front room and wrench open the front door and, having the last word, he shouted back,

"I told you, those names are not for the likes of us, no wonder they are always whining around you! The best thing I did was give them good solid names. Don't wait up."

The front door was slammed. Margery found herself shaking, and loathing her father.

Maggie also told everyone that they only saw their father once after their mother had been killed. She told them of his visit next door, and that he only stayed a short while. And during that time, he impressed upon them the need to make the most of living with the Barnes', especially as they had no children of their own. She could see that she was painting a very one sided picture of her father, and so tried to explain that this was all very common when she was a child. Men liked to have a son - it gave them credibility. "Looking back, I think my father felt Agnes was too good a wife for him. She was extremely attractive, clever, hard-working and a very talented dress maker. It probably made him feel insecure and inadequate".

Lucy interrupted,

"Granny, what happened to your father, did he survive the war?"

"Lucy, in all honesty I don't know. He never kept in touch after that last visit. That was another reason for not selling this house. After Edith and Edward moved to Harrogate a family moved in. I can't remember their surname, but they only lived there a few years. Then

Christine Friend

Jean and Robert moved in. I let both families know that I had been evacuated there, and should they ever receive any enquires regarding Margery and myself, then to let me know – in case my Dad, or anyone else from our past, tried to make contact. As far as I know, no one ever did."

Getting up from the sofa, Maggie went to the sideboard and opened the top drawer. Inside the drawer were two A5 brown envelopes, one each for Ginette, and Michael. She went and sat down again, then continued to speak.

"I don't think any of you have realised how late it is, but it is past mine and your Father's bedtime".

Lucy looked down at her watch, it had just turned 2am. She couldn't believe how quickly the time had gone. Granny must be feeling exhausted, she had probably been speaking for the best part of eleven hours. Lucy looked up to hear Maggie say,

"When Margery passed away, she left her whole estate to me. This was mainly made up of her inheritance from Edith after the Solicitor had paid her nursing home fees and it had gone to probate."

Michael raised his arm to attract Maggie's attention.

"Yes Michael."

"You haven't mentioned Margery's funeral costs?"

"No I didn't but as you have asked...In Margery's will, she wanted her funeral costs to come out of her estate. There was nothing I could do about that. So once her estate had gone to probate, and then passed on to me, I then covered all the cost of the funeral by adding it to her estate, and then dividing the whole

amount into two. I then opened two post office savings accounts. Then, when Ginette and you each turned sixteen I transferred the money into a building society account. Since then, the original building society has amalgamated a couple of times, but inside these envelopes you will find the passbooks, and your rightful inheritance from your mother."
She passed the envelopes to Ginette and Michael. Michael had the good grace not to open his.
"Now, I am very tired. Michael, you can go up when you like. Ginette, would you like a cab or are you going to walk? Looking at Roger, he seems far too tired to drive."
"Mum, we will walk. It's a nice evening - or - morning, and I think I would like to stretch my legs. We will be home in fifteen minutes."
With that, Ginette stood. As did Roger and Lucy. They said goodnight to Michael, and then in turn gave Donald a hug. But the biggest show of affection from all three of them was for Maggie. Not only was she hugged, but each kissed her, hopefully trying to convey their love and support.
Walking along the quiet streets, Ginette, Roger and Lucy whispered to each other. Ginette was wondering what had sparked her parents to tell them such a revelation, but Roger knew. He looked at Lucy, and winked. He didn't think it fair to put his daughter on the spot, and Roger was well aware that his wife would not ponder this question for long.
As soon as they reached home, they went into the kitchen. Lucy asked who wanted a glass of water.

Ginette, remembering the envelope Maggie gave her, took it out of her handbag. Roger got three glasses out of the kitchen cupboard and Lucy filled them. Ginette wasn't aware of what was going on. She was staring intently at her envelope, and then she broke the silence.
"I wonder if there are any photos of Margery? I suppose Dad would still have their wedding photos. Although, if they are as identical as Mum said then I'm not going to see any difference. A glass of water, lovely, I do feel a bit dehydrated. Roger, shall we go up now. I am beginning to feel a bit muzzy headed. Goodnight Lucy. Don't stay up too late."
Ginette and Roger were walking towards the hallway.
"Goodnight Mum. Goodnight Dad. I am going out for the day tomorrow with Marcus, so I'll try not to wake you, and I am not staying up. I shall finish this glass and then top it up and I'll be up."
When Lucy got up to her room she checked her mobile for any messages. She hadn't looked at it since lunchtime. There were a couple of messages from her friends asking if she were free that evening, and there were two from Marcus. The first one was the rugby score, and to say that he had enjoyed his afternoon with his Dad. The second showed his very caring nature. He guessed, as Lucy hadn't replied to his first message that the family meeting was still in progress. If Lucy didn't get back to him before 11pm then he would come over for 10.30am instead of 9.30am as she would need that extra hour in bed. They could decide what they wanted to do when he was there. He

wished her a good night. How generous Marcus was, and Lucy felt that she could easily tell him now how much she truly loved him.

## *Chapter Thirty Three*

When Lucy woke the following morning, the sun was bright in the sky. She looked at her bedside clock, it was just after 9am - plenty of time to get ready and have some breakfast. She couldn't hear her parents moving around the house, but they rarely slept in, and could be having breakfast in the garden on such a lovely morning.
She went to her bathroom and ran herself a hot bath. So much had been said the day before that she just wanted to lie in the hot water, close her eyes, and try to remember.
After the hot soak she felt better. More relaxed, and wondering, more than anything, how Maggie was feeling. She may have told her secret, but had that completely unburdened her and Gramps? She was also hoping that Uncle Mike wasn't causing a problem by asking too many questions. She dried and dressed in another of her new retro summer dresses, and went downstairs for some breakfast. To her surprise, neither of her parents were downstairs. She made some toast and tea and was glancing at the Sunday newspaper when her father appeared. Lucy thought looking a bit worse for wear.
"Hi Dad, where is Mum, is she is alright?"

"Good morning Lucy. She's fine, having a shower at the moment. I said I would get the kettle on and make the tea."
"There is still two cups in this pot, sit down and I'll pour you one out. Dad, thanks for not giving the game away last night. It was me that prompted yesterday, but I don't want Mum to think I have gone behind her back. It's just that I discovered something that I thought Granny should hear about first."
"I understand, and so will Mum. But at the moment there is probably still more for Mum and Mike to learn, so just leave it until the time is right."
"Thanks, Dad."
Just then, Ginette walked into the kitchen. When Lucy looked at her, she realised that nothing ever seemed to bother her mother. It was as if it had all gone right over her head.

At 10.30am the doorbell rang, and Lucy went to let Marcus in. They left shortly after 11am and decided to go to Bletchley Park. Marcus had heard some interesting things about the people who had been working there, during the war, as code breakers.
It wasn't until they went and bought some lunch, that Lucy told Marcus of what had happened the day before. He was a very good listener and never interrupted, which made it so much easier for Lucy, as she knew that she had to concentrate - there was so much to say. Eventually she stopped speaking, and was waiting for Marcus's reaction when a little boy on the

next table started to speak to the elderly gentleman sitting with him.

"Great Grandad, what bit did you work in?"

"I never worked here. You had to be very clever, and anyway I wasn't old enough. I was a child during the war, and because we lived in Walthamstow and my Mum and Dad were worried about the bombing, I was evacuated."

"What's that Great Grandad?"

"It's when the children are sent to live in what everyone hopes are safe places. That could be in the countryside, or in a village, or even a town, far away from London and other big cities. Then when the war was over, you went back to your Mum and Dad. I was lucky, I went to a place called Finedon in Northampton."

Lucy turned around in her chair and spoke to the elderly chap,

"I am sorry for interrupting, but my Grandmother was evacuated. She lived in Stepney and was sent to St. Albans."

The gentleman was clearly interested in what Lucy had to say, and turned his chair to face her.

"That's a nice part of the world to be evacuated to. Did she ever go back to St. Albans?"

"Well actually, she never went back to Stepney. Her mother was killed during the blitz, and her father was away in the navy. She doesn't know what happened to him, so her and her twin sister stayed with the couple they were evacuated with until after the war had finished."

## When Life Changes Direction

He was rubbing his chin, as he answered,
"That's a sad story. I was evacuated with my sister. My Mum told us that we were to be billeted together, but when we got to be picked there were two couples who could only take children of the same sex. My sister went with a girl in her class, and the girl had a brother in mine so we went together. The couple we were billeted with were shoe makers, and they had their own little work shop at the bottom of the garden. My friend and I could always be found down there watching the shoes and boots being made, it fascinated us. I can tell you, I enjoyed the freedom - no older sister to watch over me!"

Lucy, Marcus and the elderly gentleman were all laughing.

Lucy was intrigued with his story, and so wanted to know more.

"What happened to you, did you stay the whole length of the war?"

"No, my sister didn't enjoy it, so she wrote and told my Mum, and the next thing I know is my Mum came up to Finedon and took us back home. We were away for about three months, but of course once I was back home it was lovely being with my Mum and Dad again. You know it wasn't the same for all children though. Some were billeted with terrible folk, whereas some had better lives than they did at home. The family that one of my friends went to wanted to keep him at the end of the war, and he wanted to stay. He had a much nicer life once he was evacuated, but his parents wanted him back and so back he went."

The little boy, who had been listening the whole time, looked up and called out,
"Nanny, Grandad, we are over here! Great Grandad's been telling us about the war."
The couple came over and smiled at Lucy and Marcus. The Elderly chap stood and took the little boy's hand, and said,
"I hope your Grandmother has had a nice life. She has deserved it. 'Not right for any child to be brought up in a war."
Lucy replied,
"I really think that on the whole, she *has* had a nice life, and thank you for talking to us. It has made me understand more of what she went through, thank you."
They said goodbye, and Lucy started to feel a little emotional.
"Marcus, have you finished? Can we go outside, I need a little fresh air."
Once they were outside they continued looking around. By four o'clock, Lucy was beginning to lag, and although there was still more to see, they decided to leave it for another day.
Back in the car, Lucy stretched out her legs and fell asleep. She awoke when they were ten minutes away from her home.
"Sorry Marcus",
 she laughed,
"How rude was that - I must have been so tired. I haven't fallen asleep in the car since I was a child."

## When Life Changes Direction

Marcus parked on the driveway and they walked straight through to the garden, where her parents were laid out on sun loungers.
Lucy called to them,
"Hello, we're back. Dad, you should go to Bletchley, you would be really interested. We spoke to this chap who had been evacuated in the war, just like Granny. He was ever so interesting. It made me realise how horrible and sad it must have been for Granny and Margery."
Ginette got up off of her lounger, and offered to make a pot of tea. Once they were all sitting down and the tea had been made, Ginette told them of her brother's phone call,
"Uncle Mike phoned this morning after breakfast from Granny and Grandad's, and he wants to know if all four of us are free in two weeks for Sunday lunch. It's on him and he wants to introduce Liz to us."
Lucy was drinking her tea and nearly choked on it.
"Uncle Mike is going to introduce us to one of his girlfriends, this must be really serious!"
"Lucy, that is exactly what your Father said. Anyway are we all available."
Three heads nodded yes, and Ginette went indoors to ring her brother and let him know.

## *Chapter Thirty Four*

Donald

Having felt relieved that the secrecy that had surrounded his marriage to Maggie was now over, he still felt an inordinate amount of guilt. What would his children think of him? He certainly hadn't come across as a loving and caring husband while married to Margery.

Hindsight is wonderful thing, but it can never change anything. Within weeks of marrying Margery, he realised that he had made a huge mistake. To start with, they had never really spent any time alone. Initially when they met in the library, it was on a work level, but looking back Donald realised that his short monthly trips home seemed almost to be chaperoned. Once they were engaged, there always seemed to be some form of arrangement for the wedding that needed to be decided. Whether it was flowers, the church, or the wedding breakfast, Donald never seemed to have Margery alone.

What he hadn't noticed until they were living in Nuremberg, was how shy she was. He could understand that some of his colleagues wives could appear very confident and perhaps, intimidating. Also, most of them were a lot older than Margery. There were a few that were nearer Margery's age and they did try and take her under their wing, and they were making progress. But after three months of marriage she became pregnant with Ginny, and used her pregnancy as an escape from all social functions. Aunt Edith came and stayed for a few weeks half way through her pregnancy, but she couldn't persuade Margery to join in more. As Donald became more desperate to make his marriage work, he invited Aunt Edith to live with them. He had to admit that he was somewhat relieved when she turned the invitation down.

Then unexpectedly, Aunt Edith died a couple of months after Ginny was born. The three of them flew home. Donald, on compassionate leave. They organised her funeral, and when it was time to fly back, Margery insisted that she remain behind to clear the house. It was agreed that he would come back for her in three weeks, but Margery enjoyed being back in England on her own with the baby. She eventually went back to Germany four months later, and only then because the house sale had been completed.

Nothing changed, Margery had managed to alienate herself further from the other wives after her time spent away in England. There were never any arguments, because they never really had much to say to each other. Then miraculously, Margery became pregnant again, and this pregnancy she enjoyed. It was as if she could hide behind her baby bump. Michael was born, but then they were back to where they were before the pregnancy again, two adults bringing up two children, but living as strangers.

## Christine Friend

It was so easy for Donald to agree to Margery's idea of her going back to England to have her operation. Even the long convalescence made his life easier, almost enjoyable. The au pair and nanny could cope with the children, and no awkward questions were asked of him at work.

Waiting at the airport for her plane to land, he was dreading seeing her again. But when he saw her, couldn't believe the transformation. Could an operation cause such a change? She was confident but, not only that, happiness seemingly poured out of her. She held her head high and, for the first time, he thought how glamorous she was. He felt like he was on cloud nine. And then, when they were back in the flat and she went to change, he saw behind her ear. There was no scar. He thought perhaps he had mistaken the side it was on so, very carefully and discreetly, he checked the other ear. There was definitely no scar. This wasn't Margery. But who was she? Her voice was the same. Her laugh. She was identical in looks and mannerisms.

When he confronted her, Maggie told him the truth, that Margery had been battling cancer and had died, he was distraught. And then he became angry - very angry. His anger wasn't just at Margery, but at himself. How could he not have known what she was going through. He was happy not to travel back to see her, and instead just speak daily on the phone. He was angry again for never even having been told that she had an identical twin. Edith had briefly mentioned that there was a sister, but she made it out to be as though Maggie was a bad lot.

Once Maggie had told him the whole story, she didn't have the courage or the confidence to continue with the deceit. For her it was all over, and all she wanted to do was to return to England and be herself. Donald knew he didn't want that, but he didn't know why. He did realise that he had to grieve, and so did Maggie, and when they were on their own that is exactly what they did.

Donald went to work as normal. Maggie slipped into the life of a civil servant's wife, and then in the evenings, they cried together.

By now it was December, and a very busy month for a civil servant living abroad. Maggie wasn't in awe at the business functions they had to attend, and it gave her an opportunity to wear creations from her own shops. Donald by now realised that he could totally trust Maggie, and so each engagement became a joy to go to. The last social engagement for the December calendar was a more private occasion, held at a very opulent hotel. It was a private function, purely for civil servants and wives. One of Donald's colleagues, who always liked to be centre of attention, happened to drink more than usual on that particular evening. Maggie and Donald were sitting at the same table as he and his wife. As soon as the dancing started, with a quick step, Donald's colleague took Maggie by the hand and led her to the dance floor. He held Maggie very close, and anyone watching could see that Maggie was very uncomfortable. That was the moment that

Donald realised that, somehow, he had fallen in love with Maggie.

Donald could barely look at Maggie for the rest of the evening. He knew he was speaking to her badly, but he felt so angry with his colleague, and disappointed in himself. It wasn't until they got in the chauffeured car taking them home that Maggie asked if he was alright. He dare not answer in the car, and waited until they were in the bedroom of their flat. The bedroom that had single beds. As if it were that of a brother and sister.

It was then that he confessed to her that he couldn't go on with their pretence any longer. It would be better for her to go back to England, and then at a suitable time he would go on leave, then announce that Margery had died.

Maggie was devastated. She had also gone through the transition of grief to love, and was just waiting for a suitable time to tell Donald. She broke down in uncontrollable sobbing. Eventually she stopped, and when she looked up at Donald, and he saw the heartbroken look on her face, he knew that she felt the same way towards him as he did her.

They agreed that night to take things slowly, but back in England, and spending Christmas in St. Albans with Connie, their resolve faltered. On New Year's Eve, Donald proposed and Maggie accepted. By New Year's Day they agreed the single beds in Germany had to go to be replaced by a matrimonial bed.

Donald told his colleagues that Margery was sporting a new engagement ring, because at long last he could

afford something a lot more expensive. He also let it be known that Margery had always liked being called Maggie, as it sounded so much more friendly.
On the first anniversary of Margery's death, Donald went to visit his late wife's grave on his own. He talked to her, and begged for her forgiveness. And then thanked her for sending her sister to him. He promised that she would never be forgotten, and told her that her promise was safe. He just hoped that one day he and Maggie could be honest with Ginny and Michael.

## Chapter Thirty Five

Margery's Story.

The excitement of being engaged, and the arrangements of our wedding, made my heart dance. Never ever did I dream that someone like Donald would want me to be their bride.
I should have written immediately to Maggie to tell of my engagement, but I didn't. And then in the May, Connie wrote to Aunt Edith with dreadful news of Maggie's operation and the death of Penelope.
I suppose thinking back, if I hadn't been feeling unwell and come home early from work that day to hear the terrible row between Aunt Edith and Edna, would I ever have even been told about Maggie?
The row started when Aunt Edith realised that Connie had written to Edna as well. She insisted that Edna wasn't to mention it to me. Edna's response was to tell Aunt Edith exactly what she thought of her and her secrets, and that after all the years she had worked for Aunt Edith she was packing her bags and leaving straight away.
Aunt Edith did allow me to read Connie's letter, but made it quite clear that any contact with Margaret would definitely ruin my wedding. Donald was such a good catch. It would be very silly to get involved. How could I have been so weak.

When Life Changes Direction

Our wedding took place and we honeymooned in Torquay, the English Riviera, before we left for Nuremberg. I had no idea that there would be so much socialising being married to a civil servant. It didn't take me very long to realise that I had listened and paid too much attention to Aunt Edith's ideals of marriage, and that I had made a huge mistake.
Uncle Edward was always very sweet to me. I was totally unaware that he was unwell, so when he died it was a terrible shock. Especially when realising that he was never going to see the baby that I was now carrying. A few months after Ginette was born, Aunt Edith died and we were able to go back to England. The four months I spent there with Ginette was heaven. No one bothered me, they all thought I was grieving for Aunt Edith, and I was, but I was also relishing the life I had on my own with my baby.
When Donald came to take us back to Germany, I went with a very heavy heart. He had employed a nanny for Ginette so that I could take up my social position as his wife.
Somehow, I became pregnant again, and used my condition to escape as much socialising as possible. After Mickey was born, Donald suggested we had an au pair as well as a nanny, and that way their hours could overlap. Donald had had a number of promotions, and we had also moved to a much bigger flat so there wasn't a problem regarding cost or space, so I agreed.
By the time Mickey was six months old, I knew I should see a gynaecologist but I just couldn't bring myself to

do it. I just hoped in time that the problem would remedy itself. Of course it didn't, it just got worse, and nearly a year later I made the appointment. Looking back, I think I realised that the diagnosis could be bad. As soon as the gynaecologist had recommended a hysterectomy, he clearly pointed out that I should have seen him a lot sooner.

Donald was very busy at that time with work, and it gave me some thinking time. I had never managed to pick up much of the German language even though Donald was fluent, so I used this as an excuse to have my surgery in England. The arrangements were all made to go into a private hospital in London, and transfer to a nursing/convalescent home. The London hospital, I was happy with. But I did insist that the home should be in Hertfordshire, near to St.Albans, an area I was familiar with from my childhood. Donald agreed, and wanted to be with me for the first week. I did go along with that suggestion, but I kept thinking back to the grave look the gynaecologist gave me, and I changed my mind and asked Donald to give me some time to get over the operation, and then come and see me for a few days. It was probably the first time in our marriage where I made a proper decision. Donald agreed, although I know he wasn't completely happy. The day I left Germany, I insisted Donald went to the office and that the nanny carried on with all her normal duties. When it was time for me to leave for the airport, I was the only one left in the flat. It was best that way, just slipping quietly out of everyone's lives.

When Life Changes Direction

My biggest worry was that Donald would be told by the hospital of my diagnosis. It was explained to me that that was not hospital policy, and I would be informed first of my diagnosis. Donald would only be told of my recovery from the surgery.

Two days after my operation the surgeon came and saw me. It was to be a short consultation. How long does it take to tell someone they have two to three months to live? I had left it far too late. The cancer had spread. I thanked him for his honesty.

Donald visited near the end of my first week in hospital. He could see I was distressed. I made him believe it was because I didn't like him seeing me in such a poor state, so he went back to Germany to await my return once I had fully recuperated.

I had plenty to think about, and to plan. All my life I had sat back and let everybody else make decisions for me, now it was my turn to make decisions for other people - life changing decisions.

The idea for Maggie to change places with me was not a new thought. Very early on in my marriage, at one social event or another whilst I would be standing alone like a wallflower, it would cross my mind that Donald had married the wrong twin. During the flight to London, the idea started to grow and take shape.

The second week of my hospital visit was a very busy one. Fortunately, the hospital staff were great. When I asked if it were possible if a large thick notebook could be obtained no one questioned my motive. I was still in a lot of pain and discomfort from the surgery, but as I had already started to experience pain even before my first gynaecologist appointment, it was something that I was used to coping with.

At this stage, it had never entered my head that Maggie may have married, and possibly had a family. After all, she could have adopted? Somehow, I thought that had she done that, then she would have contacted me. Maggie had never been a secretive person, and I began to think that maybe I was.

The notebook was imperative. In it, I needed to list everything about my life. My family, Donald's work, our finances, our marriage, my likes and dislikes - everything. It was quite a monumental feat, and it was proving to be very tiring.

Once I had moved to the nursing home I made contact with the Solicitors office that had overseen Aunt Edith and Uncle Edward's move to Harrogate. They appointed a very nice Solicitor to come and see me in the nursing home. His speciality was wills and probate - ideal. He also helped me open a new bank account and transfer all my savings into an account in my maiden name. After I had seen Mr Feathergill, it was time to contact Maggie.

It was shocking to think that she didn't know who I was when I phoned, because I gave my married name. When I explained I needed to see her urgently, she came and saw me that very day. As she walked across the lawn, I could see she hadn't changed. She turned heads, something I had never done. She was glamorous, but in a totally modest way. She did have a worried look on her face, and that made me feel very sad.

The last two days have been emotional, and I am feeling scared. How could I have been so thoughtless in letting it slip that I had known about her surgery and Penelope's death? The nurses are concerned about Maggie's departure, they have recognised that since her visit, my health has deteriorated.
My last chance. I wrote to Maggie and apologised about my behaviour five years ago, and begged her to come and see me again.
The following Saturday, Maggie came to visit. She had forgiven me. We had a lot to discuss and Maggie had a lot to learn. From then on she visited every day. Not always did we discuss 'the plan', sometimes we simply talked as sisters should. Some days, Maggie had to ask intrusive questions and I would have to overcome my shyness. She constantly watched me for any mannerisms I may have. There were times when we were each insistent on doing things on our own terms. Maggie wanted Donald to know that she was my twin sister and not live a lie. I just couldn't agree to that. If he knew I had been so deceitful, would he trust my identical twin sister? Maggie was insistent that she couldn't consider selling her business until she was completely happy with her new life. Her business would be kept as a bolt hole if Germany didn't work out.
I just knew it would work out, I just knew it.

## *Chapter Thirty Six*

On Monday morning while Lucy was sitting in the office having her first cup of coffee of the day, she was wondered how her grandmother was. She didn't feel it was her place to phone her. It seemed to make a bit of a thing of it when it really should be her own mother ringing, and unfortunately, Lucy couldn't think up any other reason to call. She was also hoping to get her Grandmother alone. There were a number of questions that she had thought of, but they were her granny's private business. She decided to leave it a couple of days and hope for some kind of inspiration. She needn't have worried. On Tuesday night while she was putting a pile of clean clothes away, her mobile rang. Picking it up, she saw it was her grandparents land line, and as they hardly ever phoned her mobile from this number, she went and closed her bedroom door.
Lucy answered,
"Hello"
"Hello Lucy, it's Granny. I wanted to speak to you privately, is that possible at the moment?"
"Hello Granny, yes, I am in my bedroom and the door is closed. Is everything okay? are you okay?"
"Yes I am fine, and so is your grandad. Look, I am sure that on Saturday there were some unanswered questions for you. We don't want to leave things like that but, neither your grandfather or myself think that

it is necessary to tell the whole family unless they themselves want to know. Uncle Mike has already said to us that he doesn't wish to discuss it any more I will speak with your mother, but knowing her as we all do, she probably thinks that far too much was already said on Saturday I'll check with her, and if that is what she says, I will check that she has no objections to you continuing to your research with Grandad and me."

"Oh Granny, that would be perfect! Yes, there are some things I am curious about, and yet they could be very personal questions, questions which no one *really* has the right to ask. So if that happens, I won't feel upset if you tell me that you can't answer."

"Lucy, I am sure that won't happen but, thank you. I will phone your mother tomorrow, and then we will make arrangements. Just one more thing, has your mother said anything to you about Saturday?"

"Yes, but she has only mentioned it the once, and that was because she was saying how she would like to see a photo of Margery."

Lucy felt awkward in saying this, it made her feel a little disloyal to her Grandmother.

"Lucy, that's good. I was hoping someone would ask. Grandad and I had got out all of the photos of Margery, and her and Grandad's wedding album on Saturday, but I was so tired that there just wasn't enough time to show you all. I shall ask her here, and show her the photos on her own. It may be better to show her the photos on her own, I think it could be very emotional for her, and in some ways she is very private, just like Margery, her mother."

Lucy could hear the tone changing in her grandmother's voice, so she quickly answered, "There is no hurry, ring me when you are ready. And, Granny..."
"Yes, dear?"
"Love you."
"Love you too, Lucy. Goodnight."
"Goodnight Granny."

## *Chapter Thirty Seven*

The summer was one of the best that Lucy could remember, certainly since she had worked in the city. Another day that no jacket or rain coat needed. It was 5.30pm, and she was almost home. It was nice to leave her office before 5pm, when the majority of city workers were still working.

As she unlocked the front door, she called out. There was no response, so she assumed that her mother was probably in the garden. In recent years, her mother had become quite an avid gardener, just like her grandparents. To her surprise, Ginette was in the kitchen sitting up at the breakfast bar. As Lucy entered, she said, "Hello Mum, I did call out."

Ginette continued to stare ahead, she didn't answer. Lucy walked around to the far side of the breakfast bar so that she was now facing her mother and saw to her dismay that she had been crying. Either that, or she was suffering from a bad bout of hay fever.

"Mum, is everything okay?"

For the first time, Ginette realised that her daughter was there, and that she was looking at her with concern.

"Yes, I am alright really. It's just that this morning, I went to see Granny and Grandad. I never thought that after what we were told on Saturday that I would feel any real emotion, but they showed me some photos. I think I'm sort of upset because it was just like looking at Granny, and in my mind I keep thinking it is Granny. Perhaps if they hadn't looked so alike it would be different, but then it feels so disrespectful not to feel anything for your birth Mother?"

"Shall I put the kettle on? Would you like a cup of tea or a coffee?"

"No, nothing hot. A glass of water would be nice."

Lucy went and got two glasses out of the cupboard and filled them from the jug of water in the fridge, and then sat on the stool next to her mother. Ginette took a sip, put her glass down, and then put her arm around her daughter and instantly felt better. She then continued,

"They showed me the wedding photos. I can see why their Father could never tell them apart. They were completely identical. Edith and Edward are in the photos too. I have to say, she looked a bit of a tartar. Grandad's parents are also there, but I think it was only a small wedding. I didn't like to ask seeing as how we know Granny wasn't invited."

Just then, the house phone rang. Lucy got up to answer it,

"Hello."

"Hello, Lucy."

"Hi, Dad."

"You're home early. Is Mum there?"

Lucy looked across at her mother,

"She's in the garden."

"Can you tell her I have just got to go into a meeting? It should finish in an hour, and then I'll be on my way home."

"Okay, bye Dad."
Before she had finished speaking he had already hung up. She put the phone back and went to sit back next to her mother.
"Mum, were there any photos of Granny and Margery together?"
"Yes, there were about half a dozen. I don't think Edith and Edward could have had a camera. They were all taken by Penelope, who became Granny's surrogate mother. Actually she is in one of the photos with the twins, so I don't know who took it, but Penelope was very glamorous."
"Why don't you go and see Granny and Grandad yourself. Honestly, I am not interested in the past. Granny, to all intents and purposes, *is* my mother. She brought me up. Granny said Uncle Mike didn't even want to see any photos. He didn't want to go to the cemetery either, but she has talked him round about that. I think that once we have been, I am going to ask that it is never mentioned to me again."
Getting down off her stool, she said to Lucy,
"That doesn't mean you can't speak to your grandparents about it. I am sure there is more that Granny would like to say, but I really am not interested. To be honest, you would be doing me a favour."
With that, Ginette changed the subject.
"We have got steak tonight. I thought, salad and some new potatoes? what do you think?"
Lucy agreed, although she was now just thinking about her gran ringing to make arrangements as to when she could go and find out more about the family.

## *Chapter Thirty Eight*

Maggie didn't disappoint. That evening, as before, she phoned Lucy on her mobile. This time it was to make arrangements with her. She asked Lucy directly if she would feel more comfortable if it were only the two of them. Lucy reluctantly said that, that would be her preference, but she didn't want to upset her granddad. Maggie laughed. She knew that secretly, Lucy's grandfather was hoping to avoid yet *another* family conference. He had found it hard when Ginette had been to see them. It had made him feel like a cheat. A liar. Which in fact, couldn't be further from the truth. The arrangement was made for the following Thursday. It would give her a week to think of everything she needed answers to, as this subject had to have closure so that they could all get on with their lives. Conveniently, her grandfather would be out all day as he had already agreed to play in a golf day hosted by his golf club. After playing in the two competitions, there would be a dinner with speeches, prize giving and a raffle with big donations from local companies so as to raise money for charity. This would mean Maggie and Lucy were under no time constraints.

Once the arrangements were made and Lucy had booked her day's annual leave, she was quite excited. She had decided to take her laptop because she wanted to look for Margery's death certificate, and she wanted Maggie to be part of it.

At the weekend, Marcus was on duty, so Lucy decided to catch up with her friends. It would give her something else to think about.

On the Tuesday evening Lucy was invited by Marcus's parents to stay over, as they were celebrating their wedding anniversary, and wanted to take the young couple out to dinner. This had kept Lucy busy on Monday evening, packing an overnight bag with clothes for the restaurant and work clothes for the Wednesday. When Ginette and Roger heard of the invitation, they were both very pleased. It was becoming increasingly obvious that Marcus and his parents thought a lot of their daughter. It was nearly a year since Lucy's break up with Jake, and the subsequent heartache he had caused her.

The week had been so busy for Lucy, that she couldn't believe it was Thursday. Having been excited all week, now that the day was here, she was beginning to feel nervous, and only managed a cup of tea for breakfast. At nine o'clock, she took her bag and laptop, said goodbye to her mother, and started the fifteen minute walk to her grandmother's house.

As she started the walk, she realised that her nervousness had left her, and she was left feeling excited again. Everything in her life was starting to come together. Tuesday evening with Marcus and his parents went well. His parents were easy to be with, and although his father was a GP and his mother a headmistress, they were both genuinely interested in her job and her career plan. Lucy found this amazing, as up until that Wednesday morning, she didn't even realise that her job could be called a career! You see, five minutes after arriving at her desk that Wednesday, Mr Crawford, the solicitor that Lucy worked for, called her into his office. He asked how her evening had been, as he had heard the PA's discussing it when he walked through the office. Lucy was surprised, as Mr Crawford never discussed or asked about anyone's private life. She told him that the evening had been lovely. He said he was pleased. By now, Lucy was starting to fret that this was his way of softening the blow before she was to be fired... but then he smiled. He was pleased to let her know that she had been promoted. Instead of having one of the more senior PA's working for him, he would like to offer Lucy the job. She was shocked, and relieved! Not only was she keeping her job, but she was being promoted as well, with a substantial increase in her salary. She shook Mr Crawford's hand and thanked him, and told him that she would be very happy to continue to work for him in this new post.

Lucy was smiling to herself as she was walking along the road, thinking back over the last two days. In no time, she was walking up her grandparent's drive, and knocking at the door. Listening for the 'clip-clop' of her grandmother's shoes inside, she realised that it was only two weeks since she had first come and seen her grandmother about her discovery.

## When Life Changes Direction

The door opened, and there stood Maggie, looking more her old self. They both walked into the kitchen where her grandmother had been making coffee, and Maggie asked Lucy all about Tuesday evening. The coffee, cups and biscuits were all placed on a tray, which Maggie carried into the dining room, followed by Lucy, still carrying her laptop and handbag. Lucy sat down and placed her handbag on the floor, and her laptop on the table. She noticed the wedding album and small pile of photos next to it. Her relationship with her grandmother had always been an easy one, even when she was going through her teenage years. Lucy at times felt Maggie understood her more than her mother did, but seeing the photos brought back to her what her visit was about.

Maggie saw her granddaughter glance at the album. "Lucy, would you like to see the photos that I showed your mother, and then we can sit and talk."

Lucy nodded. The wedding album was kept until last. Lucy couldn't get over the likeness of the two sisters. She had seen a couple of sets of identical twins before at school. They were never quite mirror images, but that was exactly what Maggie and Margery were. She was pleased to see the photo of Penelope, and asked her surname. Maggie told her it was Waltham, Lucy frowned.

"What are you thinking dear?"

"Gran, I have heard that name before, really recently. I know, Lauren was telling me about her cousin who has just won a fashion and design scholarship. Her cousin is

very talented, and is so appreciative of it, and I am sure it is called 'The Penelope Waltham bursary'.
Maggie smiled.
"That's so nice to hear that a worthy person has won it. Yes, it is my Penelope. After I sold the business, I wanted to do something worth while with the money. Something that Penelope would have been proud of. She always had a lot of time for young people, and so your grandfather and I set up this trust fund in her memory. If you remember last Saturday, I told you she was wealthy, and left almost everything in her will to me. Some of Penelope's money was family money. Her parents were both killed in a train crash when Penelope was twelve. They were travelling first class in an overnight sleeper, and the following train ran in to the back of their train. All very sad, but you see, that's how Penelope knew what grief in childhood was like. She had already experienced it first hand. I think I had better start my story from the very beginning. And so, Maggie told Lucy her life history, starting with a disappointed father after the arrival of his twin daughters.
Every so often, Lucy would write something down in her notebook but, at no time did she interrupt her grandmother. Maggie explained how she knew that Edith had really only wanted one evacuee, and that she had heard the fraught discussion between Edith, the Vicar and her Headmistress. It was one of the things Maggie had discussed with Margery in the nursing home. Margery said that she had heard nothing, she was so frightened that they were going to end up with

some kind of bogey man. Maggie then stopped, and looked at Lucy,

"As your Mother has gotten older, I have realised how much she is like Margery. It is not something I can ever discuss with your grandfather, but I actually find it comforting knowing that a part of Margery lives on."
The atmosphere started to feel thick with heightened emotion. Lucy, selfishly, didn't want this to happen. She had so many unanswered questions. She looked at her watch and suggested that, perhaps they should stop for some lunch.

Sandwiches were already made in the fridge. They decided to eat in the garden under the pergola where it was cool and shaded.

Just over an hour later they were back in the dining room. Maggie was ready to pick up the tale. She began to explain how Margery's plan came to be.

"Gran, I am sorry to interrupt, but when did Grandad realise you weren't Margery?"

"I had decided to go to Germany straight after the Solicitor had handed me my envelope. I told Connie that it was a holiday, she never questioned why I had chosen Germany. I still didn't know if I was going to tell Donald I was Maggie, or pretend to be Margery at this point. In fact, when I got to the arrival hall I saw him first. He looked so forlorn and then when he saw me his face lit up, and that made me realise I couldn't let him down. I had to be Margery. He kissed me on the cheek and told me how wonderful I looked, and I could see how relieved he was for me to be there. We left the airport and went straight to the apartment where

Christine Friend

Ginette and Mike were waiting with the au pair for the family reunion. I was wearing a linen two piece with a woolly jumper underneath, but Nuremberg was hotter than England, so after ten minutes I went to the bedroom to change. As I took the jumper over my head I caught it on my earring. At that moment Donald came in and unhooked the jumper, he didn't say anything but from that moment his mood changed. He seemed to become a little distant. Remember, I had never met him before, I wasn't sure if this was just him? We took the children to the park in the afternoon and everything was going well. Ginette said she liked my shorter hair and my new clothes. It was later, when the children were in bed, that Donald confronted me. He looked straight at me and said he knew I wasn't Margery, who was I and where was she. It makes me go cold to think of it even now. There was no point denying it so I told him the truth, everything. Can you imagine how difficult that was? To tell your brother-in-law that his wife had died of cancer, and that she had suffered with it alone without, what should have been, the closest person to her. He just let me speak. He did get angry, and he was obviously very upset and shaken. It was only after I had nothing more to confess that I asked him how he had known. It was my jumper. When he unhooked my earring he realised that there was no scar, apparently Margery had a scar about an inch long. It must have happened when we were really small, I had no knowledge of it, and I don't think Margery knew she had it either. I thought the game was up. I would return to England, and he would have to

announce that Margery had died. But he said, although it was a huge ask, maybe we could we give it a try as Margery had wished. It's funny looking back now, we did take things very slowly. The sleeping arrangements were easy as they already slept in separate beds."
Lucy was beginning to feel a red glow listening to her gran telling her such intimate details, but it didn't seem to bother Maggie, and so Lucy soon forgot her own embarrassment and continued to listen.
"It wasn't until Christmas did he hold me in his arms and kiss me. Remember, I had already decided never to marry, so by this time I had had a small number of lovers. There was temptation on both sides, however we had decided to wait before becoming properly intimate. But he proposed New Year's Eve, and the waiting ended. He bought me my own engagement ring, and told his colleagues that he was now in a position to buy 'Margery' something decent. Margery's engagement ring is upstairs. I returned to England three times that year, only for about a week or so each time. There was the business to attend to. I had put a manageress in place, and she sent weekly reports to me regarding sales and stock, but I did like being hands on. More importantly, I wanted to see Connie. As Penelope was my surrogate mother, Connie was my surrogate grandmother. I had told her that I had met a widower with small children, and she knew how much I wanted a family, so she accepted my life style. Every time I left Germany, it was harder, and every time I returned, it was to be more in love with Donald. Lucy, you may not like this, and may possibly find it a bit

strange, but Donald and I married that September on the same date that he married Margery. It meant we didn't have to lie about our wedding anniversary, only the amount of years. We married in the registry office in St.Albans with office staff acting as witnesses. Connie and Edna looked after Ginette and Mike for us, and then the six of us went out for a celebratory lunch. Before you ask, Edna never suspected that Margery had ever been married to Donald but, although Connie never asked, I am sure she knew. Mike is so much like Margery in looks, and therefore like myself as well. Donald's job lasted another six months in Germany, and then he was promoted with a job in Whitehall and we moved back to this house. It was then that I sold the business. I really wanted to be a stay at home Mum. Donald was attending more and more functions where I was expected to accompany him. And as you know, I loved every minute of it. Connie still lived with us but I made her retire, and so we had daily help come in. The house was extended and then when your Mother was nine, Connie died. I found losing her so hard. She was the only person left who had known me since I was five, everyone else had gone. I was only thirty one."

The conversation was becoming a little maudlin. Lucy though it a good moment to mention to Maggie that she had looked for another marriage certificate, but couldn't find one. Maggie was surprised, and went to the study to fetch her marriage certificate.

Lucy looked at it. Everything seemed to be in order, so she suggested to Maggie that if she liked, they could look again on her Family History website. Maggie was most intrigued and Lucy explained how it worked. While she was explaining, she realised that when she searched before it was only under her grandfather's name. Thinking back now, Lucy realised how disappointed she had been at the time. What if there hadn't been a registration under her grandmother's name? Lucy knew she would have found it hard to accept that they had never married. This time, it would be easy to search with Maggie at her side. She typed in her Grandmother's name, 'Margaret Bailey'. There it was, top of the list of possibilities. She then clicked on to the transcript, 'Margaret Bailey married to a Ronald Urquhart Green'.

"Look Gran, they have transcribed Grandad's name as Ronald. Let's look at the images. It's the same."

With this, Lucy picked up the marriage certificate again and had a close look at her grandfather's name.

"Looking at it now, the writing is so loopy, it does look more like an 'R' than a 'D'."

Then looking at her Grandmother, with a cheeky grin, Lucy said,

"I hope that still means you are married."

And Maggie replied,

"Most definitely, the registrar actually said how nice it was to be marrying a Donald and not a Ronald for a change."

With this they both laughed.

"Gran, now that we all know the story, are you relieved?"

"Yes, I am. I found it a constant burden, part of me living a lie, and I felt guilty but, it was a promise I had made to Margery. Now I worry because I don't think we are out of the woods yet. It will take some time for it all to sink in for your mother and Mike. Yes, I know they say everything is fine, but let's wait and see. And for me, there are still parts of my life where there are holes.

When my mother and grandmother died, Margery and I were never told any of the circumstances. Were they killed outright, were they injured and died of their injuries, did they have a funeral? All Margery and I were told was that they were dead. Then of course, what happened to my father? For many years I hoped he would just turn up out of the blue."

"Gran, this is going to sound a bit silly but, why didn't you look for him? You know you could have hired someone, and I am sure there are some charities that are known for helping to find lost persons, or failing that, would a Solicitor have been able to give you some advice?"

"I did think about it and your grandfather was very supportive, but I was always worried that if he had made a new life for himself he may not thank me for finding him. It wasn't as if we had a close relationship. In fact, we rarely saw him. I think he enjoyed his freedom too much, and he left my poor mother looking after his own disabled mum. That doesn't sound like a very caring person, does it. And as I have already said, he told us to make the most of Edith and

Edward as they had no children. The thing is, now I regret not having done anything."

"I've got my laptop with me, why don't we see if we can find him?"

"Is it as easy as that?"

"You never know, it could be..."

With that, Lucy got her laptop out of it's case and typed in her family history website.

"Gran, what was his name?"

"He was called Tommy Bailey, but I don't know if he was actually 'Thomas' or just 'Tommy'."

Lucy had a thought,

"Well, we could try and find the registration of his birth and marriage, and then that might help us with what he was actually named."

Lucy typed in 'Tommy Bailey', and to narrow the field, put in 'Stepney' as the registration district. There was only one Tommy, but it defaulted and a number of Thomas's came up as well. Lucy tapped on to the only Tommy Bailey transcript and saw the mother's maiden name was 'Buxton'. She asked Maggie if that seemed right, but Maggie could only shrug. She could only ever remember the old lady being called 'mum' or 'Mrs Bailey'.

"Why don't I order the certificate. Who knows, it may be the same house that you were born in? Let's look now and see what name he put down on their marriage certificate."

Lucy now went to marriages, and put 'Tommy Bailey' in, and this time added the year from the birth registration. Again, only one Tommy Bailey appeared.

But when she went to the transcript they could see the name of his spouse, 'Agnes Pollard'.
Maggie shouted,
"That's her, that's my mother! I always thought Agnes was a horrible, plain name. Can we order that certificate as well?"
"No problem, let's look now and see if we can find a death certificate. You are alright to do this..."
"Look Lucy, I think it's time I knew, don't you."
Back to Lucy's laptop and she now searched the deaths again, putting in 'Tommy Bailey' but removing the district of Stepney as it was possible that he could have died anywhere. This time four Tommy Bailey's appeared. Two of them Lucy ruled out straight away, as their deaths were both during the Great War. That left two. One of the deaths was registered in Loughborough, Leicestershire, and the second one was Plymouth, Devon. When Lucy looked at the transcript for the Loughborough registration it belonged to a baby. Plymouth was the last of the four. She went to the transcript the year was 1942, the fourth quarter, and it had the correct age for Tommy at that time.
"Gran, I will order this certificate as well, if it isn't him we will find him, and if I can't then we could always seek help from a professional genealogist."
Lucy didn't want to raise Maggie's hopes, but if her great grandfather had been in the navy then, didn't Plymouth sound feasible?
It was now five o'clock, and Lucy felt that she had done more than a day's work. Maggie had been totally open

and honest, and at the moment Lucy really couldn't think of anything more she needed to ask.
"Gran, shall I make us a drink? I think we both need it."
"Yes, that sounds like a good idea. I would like a gin and tonic. What time are you expected home?"
"I didn't want to put us under any pressure and Mum and Dad are going to a Garden club meeting tonight so I can please myself."
"What about Marcus?"
"He is on night duty. I won't be seeing him now until Sunday morning. I don't know what it is but, if I hadn't been seeing Jake for a couple of days I would have panicked, but with Marcus it is totally different."
"Lucy, that is called trust."
That night as Lucy was getting ready for bed, she couldn't help thinking about Tommy and that if it wasn't his death registered in Plymouth, where was he? And why didn't he ever contact his daughters again?
As Lucy was thinking about her great grandfather, Maggie was thinking about Lucy. There was one question Maggie had been dreading Lucy asking, and that was 'did any of the wives of Grandad's colleagues notice a difference?' If she had asked, Maggie wanted to tell the truth. The wives had become Maggie's friends within a few months of her arriving in Germany. They all had thought the hysterectomy had turned Maggie's life around. They couldn't believe the transformation, and all said if only they had known how much she had been suffering that they would have encouraged her to get help sooner. They were all

astounded with her new found confidence, it would certainly help Donald. After all, the job had a lot of socialising and the last thing a man needs is a wallflower for a wife. This though, was about Lucy's grandmother and would have been disloyal of Maggie, and she knew this. Luckily Lucy hadn't asked, otherwise it would have had to have been another lie.

## *Chapter Thirty Nine*

That Sunday was to be Mike's big day, introducing his new girlfriend. The family had, in the past, occasionally met Mike's girlfriends, but they never lasted. They never saw the same one twice.

Right now, Maggie was feeling bothered by what had happened the day before. Mike had phoned Maggie on the Friday asking if she would come with him and Ginette to the cemetery on Saturday if she was free. He had said he knew it was short notice, but it was bothering him. He didn't understand why because, he didn't have any memory of Margery. Or was it, he wondered, because he was actually getting stressed over his family meeting Liz? If he could go to the cemetery first then hopefully he would be able to cope better on the Sunday. Maggie and Ginette were both available, so Mike said he would pick them both up at 10am.

Mike went to Maggie's first and then on to Ginette's. Ginette heard her brother tooting the car horn and wondered whose car they would be in. The three of them couldn't possibly squeeze into his Morgan sports car? She was relieved to see he was driving Maggie's car. She called goodbye to Roger, picked up the large bunch of flowers and got into the back of the car with Maggie.

By time they reached the cemetery it wasn't yet half past ten, and there were only two other cars there.

Christine Friend

Mike and Ginette got out, and solemnly followed Maggie to see their mother's grave for the first time. It was as Maggie had said at the family meeting. A plain white head stone, with Margery's Christian and maiden name on it, and two dates, her date of birth and the date of her death. What seemed odd in comparison, was that the surround of the grave was not only in a manicured state, but around the plinth was planted pansies in mauve, yellow and cream. The colours looked spectacular, and the fullness and amount of the pansies almost made them look artificial. The plinth had two holes with a gold covering grid for flowers to be arranged. The three of them just stood staring down, and then Maggie spoke,
"Margery, I have brought them. They're here. Ginette and Mike. It's been a long time. I am sorry for that, please forgive me. But I kept my promise"
With that, she kissed the tips of her fingers on her right hand and placed them on the headstone. She turned and slowly walked back to her car, leaving her niece and nephew at their mother's grave. She didn't look back. She couldn't. The tears were streaming down her face. At this moment in time, she felt she was losing the bond she had with them, and not for the first time in her life, she felt totally bereft. She reached the car and with the spare set of keys, opened her car door and got in.
Meanwhile, Ginette was already arranging the flowers. Mike knew they were here due to his instigation, but he felt guilty because whatever he was expecting, didn't happen. In fact nothing happened. All he

wanted to do now was get back to his parent's, pick up his car and make the most of the day with Liz, who was waiting for him at his house. Once Ginette had finished the flowers, she said,

"Mum, I want you to know you made the right decision. Maggie was the right person to take over from you. How clever of you, and thank you. Now I know where you are, I will be here again. Love you."
She then copied Maggie's gesture. She waited for Mike to say something but then realised, what could he say? This woman was a stranger to him. She took his hand just as she did when they were little, and they walked back to the car.

## *Chapter Forty*

The following day, Marcus arrived as punctual as ever. Lucy made coffee, and they took their two cups in the garden. Although Lucy had spoken to Marcus since her meeting with her gran, she still wanted to talk some things through with him.
Ginette and Roger stayed in the kitchen giving the young couple some privacy.

Mike had decided to choose a gourmet pub for his introductory lunch, and no expense was spared, but by time they all met in the bar, Mike was extremely nervous. Ginette and Roger arrived with Lucy and Marcus. Why Mike was so nervous, no one could understand. Elizabeth, or 'Liz' as she asked everyone to call her, was extremely friendly and chatty. She was tall with long auburn hair and very large brown eyes, and older than Mike's previous girl's friends. As the conversation went on, Liz told the family that her eighteen year old son was soon going to University to study engineering. She had been a widow since Nathan was six years old, and was indebted to her parents for all the support they had given her over the years. The topic of work came up, and Mike told them all that he had met Liz, a locum pharmacist, in the chemist next door to his dental practice. He had inadvertently forgotten to sign a patient's prescription. She had phoned him and, as he had a spare five minutes, he popped next door to remedy the situation.

Maggie was impressed - brains as well as beauty. This was what Mike needed, someone to take him in hand but, in a loving, kindly way.

The lunch was a total success. By the time dessert was served Mike was back to his usual self, and was telling more of his terrible jokes.

Maggie reflected later that, perhaps she should have broken her promise to Margery and told Ginette and Mike when they were much younger adults. Or was she just lucky that they had reacted in such an understanding way?

## *Chapter Forty One*

On the following Friday morning, Lucy was at the front door calling to her mother that she was ready to leave for work. As she was waiting for Ginette to come into the hall, the letter box flap was lifted up and a pile of envelopes fell to the floor. She picked them up. Two envelopes were for her father, a holiday brochure for her mother and three brown envelopes for herself. She put hers in her bag just as Ginette arrived in the hall.
"Bye Mum, remember I'm out with the girls tonight, so no dinner. We are going to the cinema so we will eat on the way."
Ginette bent forward and kissed Lucy on the cheek.
"Have a lovely day. Look, my holiday brochure has arrived, was that more certificates for you?"
"Yes, I can't wait to open them, if I get a seat on the train I can open them then."
Lucy was out the front door and walking fast so as not to miss the earlier train.
She arrived on the platform with only a couple of minutes to spare. The train pulled in and just as she was hurrying for a seat she heard her name called. Turning round she saw it was Jessica, a girl she had been at school with.
Lucy knew it would be rude to ignore her, so she turned around and walked back to the other end of the carriage and sat next to her old class mate.

"So glad to see you Lucy, when is it you start your travels? I heard about you and Jake taking a year out."
"Who told you that?"
"One of Lauren's cousin's friends is a girl who works in my office."
"Well you will have to tell her to check her facts in future. Jake dumped me about this time last year, it's his new girlfriend that is going with him."
"Lucy I am so sorry, I didn't know, are you okay?"
"Perfectly, actually. It would never have worked and as it is, he has done me a favour, a massive favour."
As Jessica looked at Lucy she couldn't help but notice the huge smile.
" I'm now seeing a Doctor, Jess."
"A Doctor, how did you meet? has he got a brother?"
Lucy laughed.
"Sorry, an only child. But you will never guess how we met..."
Lucy spent the rest of their train journey telling Jessica how Marcus knocked into her on the nursery slopes. How she thought he caused her broken ankle, only to find out by watching YouTube that it was someone else's fault. By the end of the tale both girls were laughing so loud that a number of newspaper reading, and phone scrolling commuters were tutting.
After saying goodbye to Jessica, Lucy stopped at her favourite coffee shop and bought a take away flat white.

## *Chapter Forty Two*

At her desk she hung up her jacket, and then immediately got out her three envelopes. Slitting the first one open, she found inside a birth certificate. It was indeed, her great grandfather's. It was the same address where Maggie and Margery had been born. It also revealed that her great grandfather had been registered as 'Tommy', which Lucy felt relieved at - there was so many Thomas Bailey's she would have to have searched through.

The second envelope contained a death certificate. Whoever had supplied the information for this death had been very thorough.

In the field 'time and place of death', it stated that it was $4^{th}$ December, 1942, at Plymouth General Hospital.

Name: Tommy Bailey

Occupation: of 52 Lodge Road, Stepney, he was a naval rating in HRH Royal Navy.

Cause of death: Injuries received from an explosion aboard the HMS PENYLAN.

Lucy sat back in her chair, stunned. This was the answer her grandmother had been looking for since she was a child. He had been killed in the same year as his only visit to them in St.Albans. All those wasted years, wondering where he was and what he was doing. Lucy didn't have to cross reference the address with the first certificate, she knew it off by heart now.

Lying on her desk was her great grandfather's death certificate.
So engrossed was Lucy, that she hadn't heard Mr Crawford say good morning to her. She looked up suddenly to see him looking at her in a concerned way, "Lucy, I can see that is a death certificate you have there, whose is it?"
"Sorry Mr Crawford, I didn't hear you come in. I have just had a bit of a shock, it belongs to my great grandfather. My grandmother never knew what happened to her father, and I have just found out, and now I'm not sure what I should do?"
"Well, from a personal and professional point of view I don't think it a good idea to tell her over the phone. It would seem very impersonal. Far better to do it face to face, then you can show her the certificate as well. Can I ask when this incident happened?"
"The 4$^{th}$ December, 1942. Apparently he was aboard a ship called the HMS PENYLAN. So I now need to find more information. I was wondering, do you think the imperial war museum would be able to tell me something about the ship?"
Mr Crawford was considering his reply, the way he did with any problem before answering.
"You could contact the reference library in Plymouth, I am sure they would have records. As it is, you don't know if the explosion was due to enemy fire, or an accident aboard ship. You could also google it or try the Royal Navy, they must have a war archives."

"Thank you Mr Crawford, I hadn't considered an accident on board ship. I will make a list and tackle it during my lunch break."
With that, Lucy's desk phone rang and made her jump. She thanked Mr Crawford for his help and went into work mode as she answered the call. Her working day had now started, Tommy Bailey would unfortunately have to wait.

It proved to be a very busy morning for a Friday. Clients wanted appointments moved, and two clients who had been in to see Mr Crawford had changed their minds on various details on the contracts waiting to be signed. In some ways it helped Lucy to keep focus on her mornings work.
At eleven thirty, Carolyn, one of Lucy's fellow PA's, had offered to do a sandwich run, which meant Lucy would gain another fifteen minutes with her research.
Eventually, Mr Crawford left the office on a business lunch, and Lucy decided it was time to find out a little more about her great grandfather.
Mr Crawford had suggested googling it - that would be a start. To her surprise, a photo immediately appeared and, next to it, a wealth of information. The website clarified that the explosion was caused by a torpedo from a German motor torpedo boat, known as an 'S Boat S115', in the English Channel. The HMS PENYLAN was escorting a coastal convoy at the time. Five officers and a hundred and twelve ratings were rescued. The wreckage was protected under 'Protection of military remains Act 1986'.

Lucy didn't know whether to be excited or sad, but she decided that she would follow up Mr Crawford's other idea up and contact the reference library in the area. They were most helpful. They in turn suggested that the quickest way of finding anything out about Tommy Bailey was either to send an email, or, try phoning Plymouth's local historian.

Gordon West was a fountain of knowledge when it came to naval matters in the English Channel, and if he didn't know, then he would certainly have the means to research for her. They gave Lucy, Gordon West's email address and phone number, and wished her success in her research.

What was the best way of contacting this chap? If she emailed him she might have to wait a considerable time for a reply, and Lucy felt now there was a sense of urgency. She decided to phone, and if there was no answer, only then would she email him.

The phone rang five times, then went to an answer machine. Gordon West's voice was very clear and precise. She was to leave contact details and he would return the call as soon as he was able to.

Lucy was disappointed that he hadn't answered, but she liked the voice and felt confident that he would do just that. She left her phone number and hung up.

By now she was beginning to feel hungry. She went to the office kitchen to make herself a cup of tea and fetch her sandwich from the fridge. Back at her desk, she started to eat when she suddenly realised that she had only left her work phone number. No mobile or

home number. 'If he rings at the weekend or evening he will just think I am a time waster', she thought.
She put her sandwich down and started to write an email. This time, she put all three phone numbers down as contact details. She also explained about her great grandfather, asking if Gordon could give her any information or recommend where she could do some research herself. After reading it through twice just to make sure there were no mistakes, she pressed the send button.
There was nothing more she could do now other than sit and wait. And of course, finish her lunch.
Normally when Lucy ate her lunch at her desk she would activate her voicemail, but she forgot, and after her second bite of her sandwich her phone rang.
She had to answer it; it was office policy not to let a phone ring continually.
"Hello, Mr Crawford's PA speaking, how may I help?"
As soon as the caller started to speak Lucy recognised the voice.
"Hello, I am calling to speak to a 'Lucy'..."
But before he could finish, Lucy butted in.
"Yes, that's me! Hello Mr West, I recognise your voice from your answer machine. Thank you so much for returning my call so quickly."
This time she allowed him a chance to answer.
"I was in my garden when you called, I took note of your phone number to ring you back and then I noticed that you had sent me an email as well, so I assumed there is some urgency in your request?"
Lucy laughed.

"The urgency is only on my part. I am afraid I am being extremely impatient."
She then went on to tell him of the information that she had about Tommy. She sensed that Mr West was making notes at the other end of the phone. He didn't volunteer any information, but reassured her that he would look into her enquiry and be in contact as soon as possible. Lucy thanked him, and Gordon West wished her a good afternoon.
At two o'clock the office was a buzz again. Mr Crawford had returned from his business lunch not looking particularly happy, and more queries seemed to fall on Lucy's desk. To make matters worse, every time her phone rang she grabbed at it, hoping it would be Mr West with something of interest to tell her.

Saturday morning, Lucy was up and about early. She was going to Marcus's for the weekend, and she wanted to have a girlie couple of hours; wash her hair, paint her nails and pack a hold-all with enough clothes to last until Monday, as she would be going into work from Marcus's in Twickenham.
Marcus's parents were having a barbecue, the last one for the summer. And as Marcus was needed to help, Lucy told him that she could easily make her own way by train.
It was while her train was pulling out of Waterloo station, the last leg of her journey, that her mobile rang. The number wasn't a stored number, so no name appeared on the screen, but Lucy recognised it immediately.

"Hello Mr West."
"Hello Lucy, please call me Gordon. When I get called Mr West it takes me back to my teaching days, where the students I was addressing were never as receptive as you."
He spoke in such a kindly way that Lucy didn't feel reprimanded, and replied,
"Hello, Gordon."
And feeling a bit cheeky, asked,
"Have you any news for me?"
"Yes I have, but I am not sure what you are expecting, so I hope you won't be disappointed or upset..."

"Gordon, anything you tell me will be of help in trying to build a picture of my great grandfather's life."

"Yes, that is the right way to see it. Well I was able to track down a memorial, which has his name on it. The memorial is the Plymouth naval memorial on the Hoe. Now, I have tried to find out whether he was buried or cremated, and that bit of information I have got to wait for, but I hope what I've told you so far is of use."
Lucy was stunned. She never dreamt that there would be something that Maggie could go and see. She thanked Gordon for his help, and finished the call. She was actually feeling quite emotional, and hoped she could pull herself together before she arrived at Marcus's parents.

It wasn't until early evening that Lucy had the opportunity to tell Marcus about Gordon West. He was very attentive, and let her tell him the whole story, from Mr Crawford in the office on Friday, to Gordon West's phone call on the train.

When she had finished, Marcus could see how moved she was by all this new information, and asked her what she was going to do next.

" I haven't all the information yet. Gordon may be able to tell me whether he was buried or cremated, and where. I think it best to tell gran everything I know all at once. The fact that he died sort of exonerates him from not keeping in contact, and it may possibly make gran feel better about things. At least, I hope so".

Marcus was in total agreement, and thought that as Gordon seemed a reliable type of person, Lucy would hear from him quite soon.

## *Chapter Forty Three*

On Wednesday afternoon, Lucy's desk phone rang.
"Hello Lucy, Gordon West here. Are you busy? I can always phone you later."

"Hello Gordon, your timing is perfect. I was just about to go and put the kettle on."

"Excellent. Well there isn't a lot to add from Saturday, except that I *can* tell you that your great grandfather's body was cremated. As to where his ashes went, I am afraid there doesn't appear to be any reference. My personal opinion is that if his name was forwarded to be put on a commemoration wall, then the ashes would have been dealt with in a dignified way."
"Gordon, it is so good of you to have found out so much! I can't say I am looking forward to telling my grandmother because I am sure she will be upset initially, but not knowing is always harder I think. Would you mind if, after I have told her, and if she has any questions I can't answer, would you mind if I rang you?"

"It is always very nice to be able to use my hobby to help someone, so please give me a call if your grandmother has any questions that you cannot answer. Good luck!"
"Thank you Gordon, goodbye."

Lucy put the phone down, and buzzed through to Mr Crawford to see if he would like a cup of tea.
While she was waiting for the kettle to boil, she couldn't stop thinking of how best to tell her gran. With the tea made she knocked on Mr Crawford's door and went in. She placed the cup and saucer down and, as she did, he asked if she had made any progress about HMS PENYLAN.
Lucy told him about Gordon West, and how helpful he had been. Mr Crawford was interested in everything she had to say, and when she had finished, he asked her if she thought Maggie would go and see the memorial.
"I hadn't given it any thought. It isn't his grave, but then so many people during the war were never able to have a grave, and there is a permanent marker. It would be a nice thing to do, wouldn't it."
"Yes, I think it would be, but remember you can't influence her decision."
Lucy turned to leave his office and as she did, Mr Crawford said,
"Lucy, you have done amazingly well, I think your grandmother will be extremely grateful and proud of you."
Lucy blushed and closed the door.

When she got back to her desk, she remembered that Maggie would still be at the hairdressers, and so it was an ideal time to call her grandfather and try to speak to him on his own. Eventually the phone was answered,

"Hello."
"Hi Gramps, is Gran out?"
"Hello Lucy, yes, at the hairdressers. Did you want to speak to her?"
"Actually it's you I wanted to speak to. I have found some information out about her father, Tommy Bailey, and I was wondering when it would be a good time to pop in. I am not sure if she will get upset or not, so would you be there as well, just in case?"
"If you think she will get upset do you think it is necessary to tell her?"
Lucy felt a bit prickly about his response,
"Grandad, she did ask me to see if I could find out what happened to him. It's probably not my place to say this but if I didn't tell her, then I would be keeping a secret, and haven't we had enough of those already?"
Donald gave a little embarrassed cough.
"Absolutely right. We will be in tonight and tomorrow evening, does that suit you?"
"Tomorrow would suit me better. Tonight I can collect all my information together. See you about seven thirty, bye Gramps."
"See you tomorrow Lucy, Goodbye."

## *Chapter Forty Four*

Lucy walked to her grandparents. It was a nice evening in September. She had with her Tommy Bailey's death certificate, and some web site addresses of pictures that she thought her grandmother would like to see, and her laptop.
Instead of walking directly to their house, she made a little detour which meant she approached the house from the other end of the road. By doing this, she would walk past Edith and Edward's old house. The house Maggie and Margery were evacuated to. She had, over the years, been inside it a few times, but then it held no significance. But looking at it tonight made her feel differently. It was in this house, that Maggie and Margery saw their father for the last time, sixty eight years ago, and soon Lucy was going to tell her grandmother why.

Lucy had decided that if she started with Tommy's death certificate, then she could leave his birth and marriage certificate until last.
On reflection, Lucy was never sure if Maggie's tears were of relief or grief, but she could see the gratitude in her grandmother's eyes. Once she told her of the naval memorial on the Hoe, Donald instantly suggested Maggie should go, and Maggie insisted that Lucy should go with them. Then Lucy produced Tommy's birth certificate and marriage certificate. It was when

Christine Friend

Maggie saw her mother's beautiful hand writing in the form of her signature that she really gave way to tears. When she gained control, she explained,
"I had forgotten about my mother's writing. She used to write to Margery and I at least three times a week when we were evacuated. They were always proper letters, with funny stories in them. Sometimes they were made up, and sometimes they would be about people we knew, the neighbours or the coal man. Our milkman had a horse that would trot along nicely, but then at times he would be stubborn, and not move until he was given something to eat. Really they were about anybody who she had seen that we knew. That way, she said that when the war was over and we went home, we would know exactly what had been going on."
By ten o'clock, Lucy felt shattered. While she made the excuse of using the bathroom, she phoned her father and asked him if he would come and pick her up. She knew her grandparents would never let her walk home or get a taxi, and Lucy didn't want her grandfather to leave her gran on her own. Once she heard the car coming up the drive, she kissed her grandparents good night, and hurried out to her father.
Once in the car, Lucy and her father waved to her Grandparents who were standing at the front door, waving back. Roger looked at his daughter,
"Is everything okay?"
"Yes, it is now. I found out about gran's father, Tommy Bailey. I can tell you and Mum now, but if you don't

mind I'd rather not tonight. I feel shattered, it was quite emotional."

"I understand, when you are ready. Although I am not sure Mum will be interested, she hasn't any interest in history."

When they got home, Ginette had already gone up. Lucy said goodnight to her father and went straight up to her room. She put on her bedroom light, and checked her phone. Marcus was again on night duty, and there was a lovely message waiting for her. She replied with the same sentiment, and quickly got ready for bed. Light off, she fell asleep immediately.

## *Chapter Forty Five*

While Lucy was at her grandparents, her uncle Mike was also involved in trying to solve a family problem – well, that was how he saw it. Liz had come straight to his house after work. She was going to cook dinner while he cleaned out her car boot for her. She had been shopping the day before, and a two litre bottle of milk had leaked and had already made her car boot smell. When he had finished, she went to check it out but, instead of him being his usual jovial self he was standing by her car looking very serious.
"Mike, have you found a problem with the boot? This car has had so many little faults with it since I bought it."
He shook his head.
"No the car is fine, but I have just realised something, and I don't know what to do about it."
Liz quickly looked in the boot. It no longer smelt of sour milk. She closed the boot, locked her car, and took Mike by the hand and they walked indoors.
She dropped her keys into her handbag and then walked through into the kitchen. Mike followed but didn't speak. She turned to face him.
"Mike, is it us? Look, if it is then please just tell me and I will go, but don't drag it out."
Mike looked aghast.
"Us? No, it's nothing to do with us. Can we sit down?"

They pulled the two stools out from beneath the breakfast bar and sat down. Mike took hold of her hand and began to tell her his worry.
"When my Mother took Ginny and I to the cemetery, well, since then something has been playing on my mind. I wasn't sure exactly what it was, but tonight while cleaning the car boot, I realised. The thing is, it's a horrible subject to talk about but, what will happen when Mum and Dad are no longer here? Are they going to be buried with Margery? And if not it means she will be on her own, and somehow that doesn't seem right."
Liz knew exactly what he meant. She had also worried about this same problem. What would she do if she were to re-marry. She was in love with her first husband when he died, it wasn't as if they were divorced, but how, when the time came, could she be in two places at once?
She looked at him and smiled, because she knew it could be worked out.
"Mike, have your Mum and Dad never spoken about their wishes?"
"Wishes? No."
"Well perhaps it is because they don't know either. I had the same worry a few years ago. It was when I realised that I needed to get on with my life and, although I loved Paul very much, I really wanted to be a couple again. When Paul was buried I had a plot for two, but what if I married again? I was so worried that I contacted the cemetery. They told me that they can open a double burial plot for one more burial. Or

alternatively, you can intern ashes in the grave. Obviously there is a charge for all of that, but there isn't a restriction on the number of ashes interned. The only problems that could arise is if the cemetery, for some reason, do not allow ashes to be interned in burial plots, or it isn't possible to get the permission of the grave owner, which is necessary".

"The grave owner? I didn't know that there had to be an owner. I wonder if it is Mum?"

"Look, why don't you go and see them. After all, it is something that should really be discussed. Dinner is nearly ready. You really are a sweetie for cleaning out my car."

Before Mike rang his parents the next day, he decided to ring the cemetery. He had no idea if Liz's solution would apply to the cemetery Margery was laid to rest in. His call was answered by the most knowledgeable of people. They were extremely understanding with Mike's query. He didn't say that both sister's had been married to Donald, but did say that his mother and her identical twin sister were extremely close. They confirmed everything Liz had told him the previous evening, and were also able to tell him that Maggie was the grave owner.

Mike then phoned his parents. Maggie answered, but Mike thought her voice sounded a little flat. He asked how she was, and she told him that Lucy had discovered what had happened to Tommy Bailey. She explained that she didn't feel like telling him over the phone and he was quick to say that he could pop in that evening. If it was alright with them could it be about six o'clock before they had their evening meal. Maggie enquired as to whether he was seeing Liz later and Mike felt guilty in admitting that he was and Maggie suggested they both came over and perhaps stayed for a bite to eat. Mike realised that he would have to say why he wanted to see them so he told Maggie of his worry. He quickly added that he had a solution if there indeed was a problem. Maggie asked him if he had discussed it with Liz, and Mike said he had, so Maggie told him that there was no reason for her not to be there, "That's of course, if she would like to come?"

"Thanks Mum, I am sure she will."

Liz was flattered to be invited. After all, this was really family business, but she also knew Mike was worried about interfering in his parent's business.
They arrived just after six. Maggie didn't want to spend the whole evening on more family business, so thought that Mike's suggestion of not eating till later was a good idea. That way the subjects could be shut down. Maggie told them all about Tommy. She showed them the three certificates and also showed them photos on her laptop of HMS PENYLAN and the memorial in the Plymouth cemetery.
Mike immediately pulled the conversation around to Margery's grave, and asked them outright their wishes. Maggie and Donald looked at each other, and this time Donald spoke.

"Your Mother and I really don't know what to do. You see the problem is Margery's grave. It is a single plot. We can't get a double plot nearby, there are none available, and both of us feel that she shouldn't be on her own. That may sound silly to you."
"Dad it doesn't. That's exactly how I feel. I took the liberty of phoning the cemetery this morning to confirm what Liz told me last night."
Liz started to blush, she cleared her throat and took up the story.
She told Maggie and Donald of how she had worried about her late husband. That the cemetery had said that the solution would be that any subsequent relatives who wanted to be buried with Paul could have their ashes interned. Mike told his parents that he confirmed with St. Albans Green Park cemetery, and they could do the same.
The room went quiet and Mike looked at Liz to see if she had thought he had overstepped the mark, but when he looked back at his parents and saw tears in both their eyes, he realised they were overcome with emotion. Donald got up and shook Mike's hand, and Maggie joined in by kissing Mike and Liz on the cheek. It was agreed that Maggie and Donald would now sort out their wishes, and once it was done, they would let the family know.

## *Chapter Forty Six*

The weeks passed and it was now early November. Maggie and Donald had celebrated their first proper wedding anniversary. They had always celebrated on the right date, but not the correct number of years. It was their fiftieth, more commonly known as the 'Golden anniversary', but as they had had to celebrate it five years early, Maggie and Donald decided to play it down and celebrate it on their own.
They had also been to Plymouth. They kept their promise, and Lucy and Marcus went with them. Ginette had no interest in going, and Lucy had felt a sadness for her father because she knew he would have liked to have been included. Mike said he would probably go, but not just yet.

The weather on this particular Saturday morning in November was lovely. The sun was shining, the leaves were falling off the trees in varying shades of yellow, orange, red and green. The young couple had gone out for a drive with the intention of finding a country pub for lunch. It was a bit chilly, but a perfect November day for a drive. It was while they were looking at the menu that Lucy said to Marcus that she felt she had left Maggie with a few loose ends.
Marcus looked up from the menu, and with a frown on his face, he answered,

"You don't mean Tommy, do you? or is it her mother? You have only ever said to me that she died in the blitz. Is that the problem?"
"Yes, and I am not sure what to do. I need help, but I'm not sure where to go for it."
"Why don't you ring Gordon? He is so knowledgeable, and I am sure if he can't help then he will know someone who can. He seems to have a large network of friends specialising in some aspect of history."

.

## *Chapter Forty Seven*

The following evening, Lucy rang Gordon as Marcus had suggested. Pat, his wife, answered, and after a friendly chat with Lucy she called Gordon to the phone.
"Hello Lucy, how are you, and how is Maggie?"
"We are all very well thank you, especially Gran. She really did appreciate all the help you gave me in finding Tommy. It was so nice that we were able to meet Pat and yourself when we came to Plymouth."
"Lucy, the pleasure was all ours. Extremely generous of your grandparents to invite Pat and I out to dinner with the four of you."
The small talk over, Lucy got on to the subject of her phone call.
"Gordon, going over it in my head I still have got one piece of the puzzle missing regarding gran's family."
"Go ahead, this does sound intriguing"
"When we all met up in Plymouth, I am not sure if you were aware but Gran didn't mention anything about her mother, and it isn't because they weren't close. I think it's because she knows nothing of how she died. It's different with Tommy, she needed to know because she felt abandoned, rightly or wrongly, but with her mother I think it's because she loved her so much. I think she is afraid."
Gordon was very understanding and could see exactly what Lucy was saying.

Christine Friend

"I would like to try and find out more. Gran only knows that the Blitz started on the Saturday and on the Wednesday, her and her twin sister were being told that their mother and grandmother had died."
"Have you searched for their death certificates?"
"No, I am very reluctant to do that. What if something upsetting is written on them? I couldn't lie to Gran and say I haven't got them, but I couldn't show them to her either."
"Yes I do see that. Lucy you are a very sensitive young person a credit to your parents, and I agree that isn't the right thing to do although, if my other idea doesn't prove fruitful then you may have to resort to the certificates. My second suggestion is local newspapers. At that time most areas would have had a few weekly publications, if not daily. I feel sure that would be the best way forward. Have you heard of 'Britain's Newspaper Library', at Colindale?"
"No I haven't. Is that Colindale in North London?"
"Yes that's right, not too far away for you. It is extremely helpful and certainly worth a visit."
"Thanks Gordon, that sounds like a really good idea."

Lucy was spending the following weekend at Marcus's parents. Saturday evening they were meeting up with friends of Marcus in Covent Garden, and Sunday, his parents were taking them out to lunch. To go to Colindale on the Saturday morning seemed a lot of travelling, up into London in the morning then back to Twickenham to change, and then back into town again. But Lucy wanted Maggie to know the truth at last.

## When Life Changes Direction

As it happened, Roger was playing in a society golf day not too far from Marcus's home, and so with not too much of a detour he dropped Lucy off nice and early. Half an hour later, Lucy and Marcus were on their first journey up to town. At Waterloo they changed onto the Northern line on the underground, and finished their journey to Colindale. Within a couple of minutes of leaving the station they were walking into the library.

As neither of them had been there before they asked for help, and after Lucy had explained what she was looking for, the system of ordering up original newspapers was explained to them. Within a very short time Lucy had ordered six local newspapers for the week following the start of the blitz, on Saturday 7$^{th}$ September, 1940.

This particular Saturday morning, the library wasn't too busy, and it was still early. They went and sat at one of the reading tables and waited. Lucy felt very jittery, she was hoping this wasn't a wasted journey.

Not sure if they should be talking, Lucy and Marcus were whispering to each other when a young girl arrived at the end of their reading desk with a trolley. She had two newspapers for them, and showed them how to put them on the reading stand, and how to gently turn the page. The newspaper had overtime become very delicate, and liable to tear.

The first paper had been printed on the Wednesday for sale on Thursday. Although it was a local newspaper for Stepney, it bordered Hackney and seemed to concentrate on this area. They decided to be quite disciplined, and only glanced at the pages of dreadful images and personal stories of the blitz that filled them, and not get distracted.

Lucy was just swapping over to the second newspaper when Marcus's phone, which was on silent, vibrated. He slipped it out of his pocket and glanced at the screen. It was a work colleague. He whispered to Lucy that he should take the call and that he would go outside.

Ten minutes later, he was back in the library, walking towards Lucy. He instinctively knew that she had found something. Her face was very pale and she held a paper hankie in her hand.

"Are you okay, what have you found?"

Lucy turned the newspaper to the front cover. It was a picture of total destruction.

"Marcus, this was my great grandmother's Road. This was the damage done on the Saturday afternoon. Agnes and her mother-in-law, my great great grandmother, didn't stand a chance. There is an article inside about my great grandmother. Some neighbours of hers told the reporter all about her. It's all on pages four and five. It's very sad, but they have said such nice things about her. I have got to go to the Ladies, I won't be long. She grabbed her bag and hurriedly made her way to the toilets. Marcus turned to page four to read what had made Lucy so upset.

The large printed headline read:

## "DEVOTED DAUGHTER-IN-LAW PUTS FAMILY FIRST"

It then went on to say that Mrs Agnes Bailey, whose husband was in the navy, had selflessly stayed in Stepney to care for her mother-in-law, Mrs Sarah Bailey. Her mother-in-law was unable to care for herself properly due to the crippling arthritis she suffered from. As a result, Mrs Agnes Bailey had decided that her two five year old twin daughters should be evacuated for their own safety.

It was known by the neighbours that old Mrs Bailey couldn't manage to get to an air raid shelter, and so both women decided to use the cupboard under the stairs. Sadly their house received a direct hit from one of the many bombs that rained down that terrible day. Neither woman stood a chance. The only saving grace was that her two daughters were safe in St. Albans, Hertfordshire.

Mrs Agnes Bailey will be remembered for winning their street the award for best dressed street in the street party for the coronation of their king, King George VI. She single handedly made all the bunting and banners for the street, and decorated table cloths and various other objects. Her profession was as a wedding dress, and evening dress dressmaker. Her two little girls, named 'Margaret' and 'Margery', were always dressed beautifully. Their mother missed them terribly, but never did anyone hear her complain. The old Mrs Bailey was a lucky woman, in that her son should have married such a lovely lady.

Lucy reappeared ten minutes later. She was now smiling.
"Well I found out what I think Gran wants to know. I have just asked at the desk if it can be photocopied, and you can also have a photographic copy done as well."
Marcus turned his head to the other four local papers that were now waiting for them
"Did you want to read through these first?"
"No, everything I need is in this article. I have written down the names of the newspapers, just in case Gran might want to see them. No wonder Gran and Margery had never received any personal effects. There wouldn't have been anything left."
They ordered a photographic copy and two photocopies, Lucy paid. They thanked the staff for all the help they had been given.

Over the next few days it crossed Lucy's mind that her gran had lost so much of her child-hood. No wonder she adored Penelope, an adult able to empathise with her over her Mother's death.

## *Chapter Forty Eight*

It was nearly two weeks before Lucy's copies arrived. She had already spent time looking online and visiting all the department stores in the West End. Eventually she found exactly what she was looking for in Harrods. This was one present in which cost was immaterial. She decided on a Saturday morning to visit her gran. Her grandfather was involved in the annual general meeting of his horticulture society and so wasn't home. Maggie was also a member but she didn't get involved with the committee. If she had anything to say, then she would tell Donald her opinion and let him put it forward as his idea. Lucy rang the doorbell. She listened to her gran's footsteps on the tiled floor, and then the front door opened.

"Hello Lucy, your mum said you were on your way round."

Lucy walked in, and both ladies went into the cosy and warm lounge. As soon as they sat down, Lucy opened her bag and gave her gran the photographic copy of the newspaper pages four and five. Maggie reached for her reading glasses on the coffee table and started to read. Lucy already had a paper hankie to hand, which after only a couple of minutes, she passed to Maggie. When Maggie had finished reading the two pages, she looked at Lucy.

"Whoever wrote that article completely captured my mother. She always put everyone else first. I wish I had

been old enough to remember King George VI coronation street party. I am sure the street would have looked fabulous. Lucy, you do understand, my mother was extremely gifted when it came to sewing. Wasn't it a shame she never met Penelope. I have always thought they would have had so much in common. Now my mind is wandering. Thank you for this. I feel as though all the loose ends have been tidied up."
"Gran, there is one more thing."
"There is?"
"Yes, didn't you notice the two holes in the article?"
"I did notice them, but I didn't think they were significant."
"Gran, you were quite right, Agnes was beautiful. These are for you."
Lucy handed Maggie two parcels, both very nicely wrapped. Maggie opened the smallest parcel first. Inside, was a photo frame, and looking back at Maggie was a photo of her mother. The photo was taken of her after the street had won the competition for coronation party. It was a beautifully clear picture showing Agnes's oval face, big eyes, full mouth and masses of curly hair. It wasn't in colour, but even so her eyes were so big and her hair looking so healthy, the lack of colour in the picture didn't diminish any of Agnes's beauty.
Maggie cried, and Lucy put her arms around her.
"I am sorry Gran, I didn't want to upset you."
"Lucy, I am not crying because I am upset. I am crying because you have given me the one thing I never

thought I would ever see, a photo of my darling Mother."
She then opened the second parcel.
This package revealed a much larger, matching oblong photo frame. This time the newspaper photo, again in black and white, was of a street party bedecked in bunting, flags and banners. As she looked at the photo, taking it all in, she pointed to one of the women standing behind two very old fashioned high chairs. The toddlers had bonnets on, so their faces weren't too clear, but Agnes's was. Maggie was speechless and kept looking from one photo frame to the other. Eventually she spoke.
"I feel totally overwhelmed. I never knew that a photo existed of my mother, Margery and myself. We didn't have any photos. That would have been a luxury, one my mother probably couldn't justify".
Maggie placed the photos down onto the coffee table and took hold of both of Lucy's hands.
"My dearest Lucy, I can never thank you enough for what you have given me today. Your grandmother gave me her beloved children, and you have given me my mother and sister. But not only that, you have made me think about my father. I know I have said in the past months that he had never been very loving to Margery and myself, but you have made me think. If he had been that uncaring, why did he visit us in St Albans? It wouldn't have been an easy journey not knowing what he was going to find. When he asked us whether Edith and Edward had any children, I think he was trying to leave us in a safe place in case he didn't

survive the war. When he walked away that day he must have felt so relieved.
Due to you, I have pictures to look at and can remember my mother and Margery, and for the first time in my life, I feel at peace with my father."


That afternoon as Lucy slowly walked home, passing Edith and Edward's old home and the corner on which Tommy Bailey's girlfriend had stood waiting for him, she felt complete and total happiness. As she crossed the road, she looked back at her grandparent's home and realised how blessed she really was.

# Afterword

All of the characters in my story are fictional but some of the events mentioned did take place.

The train crash that killed Penelope's parents, on the 2$^{nd}$ September 1913 was a true event, although they are all fictional characters.

Lucy meets an elderly gentleman in Bletchley Park who relates his experience of being an evacuee. His story is the true story of my Father's (Ronald Southgate) and his sister my Aunt Betty who were evacuated to Finedon, Northamptonshire.

The events of the Blitz are true but everything relating to Agnes Bailey and her Mother in Law is fictional.

The event that caused the sinking of HMS Penylan in December 1942 is true but the character Tommy Bailey is completely fictional.

The naval memorial in Plymouth is situated on the Hoe and commemorates naval personnel from WW1 and WW2.

Printed in Great Britain
by Amazon